ALL THAT GLITTERS

A DAUGHTER OF FORTUNE, BOOK 1

DOMINO TAYLOR
VIVIENNE SAVAGE

LADY RAVEN PRESS

ISBN: 978-0-578-41012-8

ACKNOWLEDGMENTS

This is the first story I have completed on my own since I was a twenty-year-old writing *Inuyasha* fan fiction in my spare time. Over the years of working alongside my friend and co-author Alisha, I've grown accustomed to having help. It's difficult to believe I once wrote epic pieces of silly fan fic about anime characters fourteen years ago.

So, yes, for many of you wondering, this is the first Vivienne Savage novel written by only one-half of the team. I had to overcome a dozen worries—will you find me as funny when someone isn't actively laughing at my jokes as I write them?—to put this book out there for you.

This book almost didn't come out at all, and I owe thanks to the people in my digital and real life who encouraged me to continue even when I was positive I'd never get through the story on my own. Even when my mother was in the hospital and my kids were sick, and it seemed like nothing would work out, countless people convinced me not to give up.

Please enjoy this labor of love. I'm sorry for the delays and numerous times it was pushed back. May it be satisfying and worth the wait.

THE BEST THIEF

PERSPIRATION TRICKLED DOWN ROSALIA'S FACE, beading against her brow and dampening the fine strands of dark hair around her temples. Like any other day in Enimura, the oppressive afternoon sun scorched every surface it touched.

But on any other day, she wouldn't have minded, because on any other day, there usually wasn't a squad of city watchmen on her heels.

Nothing about her scheme had gone according to plan.

Anguished cries from the wronged shopkeeper echoed against stone, and she spared a glance over one shoulder to find three watchmen in hot pursuit. Swords had already been drawn, and their scarlet tabards flew behind them in the wind.

Rosalia tightened her grip on the vase tucked beneath her arm. If they caught her, they'd take it. Fuck relinquishing the reward of three dedicated week's hard work.

And thank the Five that she'd already planned the escape route in advance and greased the appropriate palms.

Six shops down, a door opened to frame a woman with an oversized pot. When she slung its contents into the alley, they missed the sewer grate entirely, and gallons of greasy cooking water sloshed against the stone path. Rosalia leapt over it then squeezed into the narrow space between the heavyset shop proprietress and the door.

Thrust off balance, the woman stumbled, flailed one hand toward the doorframe, and collapsed to conveniently fill the threshold with her considerable bulk. At the same moment, much to Rosalia's great pleasure, the first guard skidded into the greasy mess on the ground.

Were watchmen in Enimura not as crooked as they came, she would have pitied the poor sods for the injuries they sustained in the line of duty. But they *were* absolutely corrupt. As she was a paying member of the Initiated—an agent of the Thieves Guild—the likelihood was that they'd take a generous bribe to release Rosalia after her gang leader had a few words with them. It was only in the most extreme cases that thieves lost fingers these days.

Lacking time to determine if her unfortunate cohort had injured herself during the fall, Rosalia lunged from the kitchen and slammed the door behind her. She'd have to return later to thank Marta and fill her pockets with a few extra coins.

The dining hall had been cleared of all customers following the lunch rush, granting her time to shove a table onto its side and up against the kitchen door.

Precious seconds. It was all she had.

Heart pounding, she drew a flattened basket from within her cloak and shook it open. The vase went inside. So did her summer cloak and lace veil. Without eyes on her, she ripped away her tunic and stripped off her shoes. Her hair came undone, a spill of raven strands down her back, before she reached the shop door. She tossed her shoes into an empty barrel in passing and rushed outside into the summer day.

Barefoot and clothed in only a fitted wrap around her chest and loose, sand-colored pants, Rosalia fit in with most servants running midday errands for their masters. She'd even bronzed her face and body to mimic the deep golden tan most acquired during the harsh season.

Confident in her disguise, she raised the basket atop her head and blended into the crowd of faceless, nameless people sweltering beneath the sun.

Moments later, watchmen spilled out of the soup kitchen and onto the busy street. A few orders were shouted before they dispersed into the crowd, each of them running a different direction.

Exhilaration covered her arms in goose bumps despite the heat against her bare skin. She lingered between a row of stalls peddling fresh produce and flowers while waiting for her pulse to calm. Waiting for the nervous energy to die down.

When her heart slowed to a peaceful rhythm, she took a shortcut into the lower markets where the path converged into the docks. There, sea salt and baked sand greeted her—the sweet scents of home and good child-hood memories.

Her destination, a seedy, two-story tavern located off the surf, smelled like wet wood and ale. She stepped around to the rear and knocked on the back door of the Salted Pearl.

A small window slid open. "Who is it?"

Rosalia rolled her eyes. "You know who it is. Now let me in so I can have a change of clothes."

"Why do you need a change of clothes?"

"Well, for starters, I'm not wearing nearly enough."

"Or perhaps you're wearing too much."

"If you don't—"

Once the door cracked open, she bumped it the rest of the way with her hip and stalked inside. The gang's one-handed lookout, no longer capable of second-story work since he'd lost one of his hands during a burglary gone wrong, grinned back at her.

"Cutting it a little close today, weren't you? I heard the watch whistles from here. Sounded like you'd brought the whole of the city guard down upon you."

She grimaced. "It wasn't that bad, Tomli. Just a simple oversight. I didn't notice he rotates out his enchantments and alternates between the protective magic guarding his valuables. Otherwise, it would have been an easy in and out."

"Right. We all heard how easy it was."

She scowled. "They didn't come close to catching me."

"I used to think the same thing." Tomli waved his

stump and smiled. "You see what that got me. You be careful, Rosalia. Watch yourself while you're out there."

After returning his kind smile, she moved further into their hideout. The back room of the Salted Pearl had served as the base of operations for their clan for years, the home away from home for a nine-man burglary ring crammed into one alcohol-soaked den. Grinning, she crossed the dingy floor and set the basket on a table occupied by their leader's wife.

Lacherra bent over one of her ledgers as usual, a curtain of steel gray braids contrasting against darker skin. She owned the building, running a seaside inn for the thirsty sailors and travelers, though she'd met Hadrian, Rosalia's mentor, almost thirty years ago while practicing the nimble-fingered trade.

For the rich and noble, their marriage was a match made in hell. The pair had amped each other, one always putting the other up to riskier jobs and dares to pull off incredible heists. As a child, there'd been no greater pleasure than to sit at the bar and listen to tales of their exploits together. They were the two greatest thieves in all of Enimura, and no one could convince Rosalia otherwise. Even the grandmaster, the leader of all the gangs, frequently acknowledged Hadrian's great success rates.

When Rosalia neared her surrogate mother, Lacherra glanced up from her ledger and rose to sweep her into a tight embrace. "About time you made it back, girl. I thought for sure you'd come back to us like Ol' One-Hand."

Rosalia grinned. "That wouldn't be a worry if you'd

come off this lucky medallion and let me borrow it." She tapped her index finger against the gold coin dangling from a thin black cord around Lacherra's neck.

Lacherra leaned back and smirked. "You'll have to find one for yourself. Djinn-blessed gold is hard to come by. Anyway, I doubt Hadrian would let anyone harm these precious fingers."

"Where is the old elf anyway?"

"In the vault waiting for you to return with the goods. He's already found a buyer for that vase, so you'll want to get to him soon."

"Great. Thank you."

Before Rosalia could take another step, a child-sized projectile crashed into her. She stumbled back and laughed when Jabari threw his arms around her. The gang's youngest Pearl peered up at her, freckled face filled with delight. Lacherra and Hadrian were known for picking up young strays and raising them—after all, it's how Rosalia had come into their acquaintance. She'd been their orphan once too, left in their care by her mother when she was two or three.

"Hey, Jabari. How'd today go at the square?"

"Snatched enough lace and silk handkerchiefs to outfit a princess. Are you going to teach me to pick locks?"

"I did promise, didn't I? But not now. I need to see Hadrian first and handle a few other matters."

"Awww."

"I promise we'll work on it, okay? Maybe after this is done."

"Okay."

Rosalia mussed his dark hair then stepped into the stock room. Their tavern was located off the beach at the edge of a palm-shaded cove. It had been built against the jutting rocks and a trapdoor behind the bar led down into a hollow carved in the stone—a box chiseled with smooth walls where they saved casks of summer wine to conceal its true purpose. There was another room beyond it.

Her enchanted ring opened the concealed vault where they stored the gang's earnings. Their eccentric leader didn't believe in leaving it unlocked at any time, even when he was inside. Once the doors shut, it was impenetrable, unable to be opened without extraordinary means surpassing even the power of a great sorcerer. After all, a great sorcerer had created it.

She didn't want to think about how long it had taken to chisel it out or how much Hadrian had paid for the marvel to be constructed.

Inside, it was a huge space lit by two alchemical lanterns, the pale glow of their phosphorescent white-yellow light turning piles of silver and gold coins into starlight. Precious jewels winked from tiaras, necklaces, and earrings affixed to busts molded from clay. Those were Lacherra's hobby and donation to their efforts after she retired from second-story work, making phony heads to sport stolen goods.

Hadrian sat at a table near the back of the room, bent over a necklace one of the other Pearls had plucked a few nights ago from a wealthy gem merchant. He glanced up at her with a clockwork loupe in his eye and grinned,

appearing as boyish and youthful as he'd been years ago
when he brought her underwing. Such was the gift of the
elves, their eternal good looks coveted by many. "I trust
you have the spoils."

"It's right here." She lowered the basket to the table
beside his current project and dug the vase out. He'd
been prying the sapphires and diamonds from its
multiple strands to be laundered to one of their accom-
plices in the jewelry business. Later, the gold would be
melted down.

"How did it go?"

"A brief chase, nothing I couldn't handle."

"Good. Leave that with me then, and I'll have it off
on the market soon enough. There are jobs on the board,
if you're interested, and about a dozen more on my desk.
Haven't had the time to see if those all check out, but
you're welcome to do that for me too. No one else likes to
do their bloody homework these days."

Rosalia laughed and set her recent acquisition down.
"What makes you think I want to do *your* job?"

"You enjoy the challenge."

A retort died on her tongue. He had her there. "I do
enjoy it. Fine. I'll do some footwork for you."

With a step backward, she pivoted on her right foot to
return to the doorway, only for Hadrian's voice to follow
her. "Thank you, Rosalia. I can always count on you. I
owe you one."

"Don't mention it." Veering off the path to the vault's
entrance, she swung back around to the table and

touched an index finger against the top of the vase. "Actually... mind if I offer a recommendation for this?"

The elf's silver brows rose. "Have another buyer in mind?"

"No. Just... there's someone who could use a share from the profits, I think. I'd be willing to make it my share, if you're not agreeable."

Hadrian eased back in his seat and removed the jeweler's loupe from his left eye. "All right. What's this inane plan of yours, and what's it got to do with donating the share you've rightfully earned?"

As a matter of conscience, Rosalia never stole from anyone who couldn't afford it. She'd watched the artisan for days and knew he raked in enough golden ducats to feed his starving family of four, but that he kept his wife at home in a practical state of bondage. Not that anyone cared. Neither law nor nobility were concerned about the treatment of the helpless in Enimura—or the rest of the kingdom for that matter.

But this is your chance to help. To do something. What would you want if it were you? a whisper of conscience snaked through her thoughts. She'd want to be freed.

Damn her conscience and damn that asshole for neglecting the people who should have mattered most to him.

"The man has a wife, and while shadowing him, I discovered things. He beats her, Hadrian. He neglects their children. They eat scraps while he enjoys these lavish meals she's forced to prepare. And if he suspects they've had a bite or kept any for themselves, the beatings are even harder."

"And what good is a little money going to do for her if she's under his thumb?"

Rosalia crossed behind the table and tapped the map, indicating the neighboring kingdom of Nairubia. "She can leave him. We know the best smugglers in the city— on the coast for that matter. There are kingdoms beyond Saudonia where the laws governing man and wife aren't so crude."

"Or archaic." He rubbed his chin and gazed at the growing pile of gemstones. "I would be willing to make four shares of this profit instead of the usual three. One to the coffers, one for me, one for you, and one for this woman. From her coin, I'll arrange for the Saladin clan to sneak her from the city. Satisfactory?"

"Really?"

"Why not?"

Impulse threw her forward and into his arms. Despite their similar size, Hadrian caught her with ease. His chuckle stirred a few strands of her hair, and he squeezed her back tightly, with the affectionate warmth of a father. She soaked it in. Reveled in it. She'd spent too much of her childhood growing up and wanting to be just like him. Except for the part about running her own gang. That was far too much responsibility, and she preferred taking orders.

"I didn't think you would agree."

Hadrian chuckled. "Why wouldn't I? In a city where someone always wants something from me, you never ask for anything. You're my best thief and..." When he trailed off, her heart went to pounding in her chest. And what? "Well, my best thief."

His best thief? Her vision blurred a little as she parted from his embrace and straightened.

Following her, Hadrian rose from his seat, a grimace on his face when he applied weight to his damaged right leg. Even though seven months had passed since the injury, it still hadn't healed, a casualty of a trap in a wizard's tower gone unnoticed until a moment too late. Once triggered, the contraption had shot out bolts of kinetic energy and one pierced him in the thigh. "After I meet with our buyers to deliver the vase and acquire the remainder of our finder's fee, I'll present our proposal to Omara Saladin tonight. Will you make the arrangement with the wife?"

"Of course," she murmured, voice raw and eyes burning. Hadrian had never referred to her as his best thief before, merely a good thief. A *great* thief even. A talented thief, nonetheless, and a host of other adjectives, but never the best. "Send word to me when you're ready to proceed, and I'll start on these jobs."

They parted ways from the vault, each with their own tasks to perform. After all, if she wanted to lure the woman away from her abusive husband, she first had to make contact.

And put on some damned clothes.

————

Using an intermediary, Rosalia contacted the artisan's wife while the woman visited the grocer for his supper. The simple note promised help if she desired freedom from married life.

By nightfall the next day, the deal had been struck, the woman sending one of her sons into the markets with her note of cooperation. That was how easily it was done.

Rosalia used little children for such tasks. Kids in Enimura often wandered unseen and unheard, ignored while traveling the markets on errands for their parents or while loitering near the shops. No one paid any mind to the street urchins or the vagabonds unless they stole.

With exception to a rare few, there were far better ways to make use of a child's talents than to have them steal in the markets, and she compensated them well for those services. Over the years, she'd cultivated the perfect little gang to work beneath her, paying them in silver for tidbits of information and gossip seen while on the streets. A pair of little girls could play hopscotch or jump rope on a corner across from the merchant's avenue and report gossip worth their weight in gold by evening.

Once night fell the next evening, and they came closer to enacting their plan, Rosalia met personally with the woman's eldest son. He was a young man on the cusp of adulthood, nervous brown eyes darting left and right while he huddled in the shadows beneath a tailor's red awning. He mopped his brow with one shirt sleeve and glanced around, petrified.

Wary of a setup, she passed him. His shoulders slumped in genuine disappointment. He hid again, his dread radiating through the air in palpable waves. No one else stood alongside the deserted side street.

When Rosalia appeared behind him but close enough to be in his peripheral vision, using nothing more than a bit of stealth, he nearly jumped out of his skin. She raised a finger to her lips. "Shh. It's only me."

His chest heaved for a few moments longer. "Sorry, ma'am. I didn't know who to expect. Mum said your letter wanted me here and alone."

Her eyes took in his gaunt, ashen face, the sweat beading on his brow that had nothing to do with the weather—in fact, it was already cooling, a nice breeze whispering up and down the merchant lanes. A fading bruise stood out against his cheek.

"Good mother, your mum, to do what she must to keep you all safe." Rosalia set a heavy sack of ducats into his hand. His eyes grew wide, and then his gaze darted up to her.

"This is all for us?"

"Your mother's share, minus the cost of smuggling four bodies from the city. All has been arranged on her behalf as promised. Meet by the Golden Serpent at half past midnight. Tell her to be timely with the lot of you or she'll miss the caravan. Understood?"

"I understand, ma'am. What of the elixir? Mum says you mentioned an elixir to put him out so he won't see us leaving."

Rosalia produced a small vial of translucent liquid. "It is flavorless and has no odor. Pour all of its contents into his evening brandy, otherwise you *will* risk capture. The complete thing."

"Will it hurt him?"

She shook her head. "He'll fall into a deep sleep and snooze until morning. All of Opal Park could go up in flames, and he'd be none the wiser."

The boy squared his shoulders, looking a little less dead inside, and more like the man he'd have to be to help his mother and young siblings flee their father. "I can do it. Thank you."

"You're very welcome. Good luck to all of you."

She hurried away, heart a little lighter.

Being a thief wasn't all bad after all.

2

AN AMAZING CATCH

EVERY RESPECTABLE THIEF IN THE BUSINESS KEPT A day job. Hadrian and Lacherra ran a tavern at the beach, catering to thirsty sailors and dockworkers. Jabari shined shoes in the square. A couple of the older Pearls delivered packages through the city as messengers.

Despite her dearest love for thievery and stealing from the obnoxiously rich, Rosalia had another calling. In the evenings, she and her closest friend danced at the Smoke and Mirrors Theater in Enimura's Gilded Quarter, where illusion, a hint of magic, and extreme amounts of bodily control created art for the masses three nights a week. Sometimes four, if the demand was great enough and the cast was willing.

Rosalia wrinkled her nose and batted Mira's wrist. "This makeup itches."

"This is the finest makeup imported from across the Divine Sea."

"Still itches like you've smeared a handful of stinging nettles on my cheeks."

Mira settled back, exasperation whistling an exaggerated sigh from her lips. "It does *not*. And even if it does, well, maybe you'll keep on top of your belongings next time. When you don't restock your personal supplies prior to an event, you're left to the mercy of whatever *I* have on hand."

"I was busy."

"So was I. Hadrian had me crawling all over bloody rooftops and shit this week, but I still managed to respect my responsibilities in our other trade. We're dancers primarily, remember? We dance."

"It isn't as if we make more money here—"

"For Arcadian's sake, Rosalia. It isn't about where we make the most money. It's about personal duty. About your own reputation. About Frederico's reputation. You won't always be able to rely upon me to remember the things you neglect."

A lead weight plummeted to the bottom of Rosalia's stomach. "I'm sorry. I was being a brat, and you're right."

Mira swept the brush over the apples of Rosalia's cheeks and blended rose gold blush toward her temples. "I know I'm right."

"So what is this stuff anyway?"

"It's clay harvested from the shores of Oceana and infused with pigment," Mira explained. "It doesn't budge, even if you sweat beneath those enormous spotlamps while surrounded by all of Anura's pyromantics."

There couldn't be a more brilliant set designer than

Anura. Somehow, the older woman turned sorcery into a thing of art, combining enchantments and technology to create masterful designs that brought their stage to life. The Smoke and Mirrors Theater wouldn't have its reputation without her. Customers came as much to see the spectacles of magic as they did the dancers.

"Rosalia!" the stage manager called. "You're set to go on stage in five."

Mira shooed her. "I'm finished with you. Go."

This was showtime, the best time of the night, and honest paying work that kept the suspicion off her lifestyle when she wasn't on the stage. As a dancer, she was paid well, earning three to five golden ducats a week for her performances. Two ducats were enough to shelter, clothe, and feed a single woman in comfort, but with her earnings, she could afford the finer things in life—beautiful veils, silk dresses, hand-painted scarves, and other wonders. She kept herself adorned in paints and the flourishes of modern fashion and played the courtship game with the young suitors who tried to visit her after she'd left the dressing room.

At least she *had* participated in the courtship game. About six months earlier, one of their regular visitors had wanted to speak to her in person to make a marriage proposal. He'd waited until the other girls had emptied the dressing room before sneaking inside, and once there, he'd cornered her, demanding for her to accept the attention he'd supposedly been attempting to lavish upon her for weeks.

The confrontation ended with her hair comb embedded in his carotid artery.

She'd claimed to the city guard that it was an accident, just a blind, terrified thrust. After that incident, Frederico had hired additional bodyguard staff to block overassertive admirers who wouldn't take no for an answer.

Because it was better than a dancer drawing attention to herself a second time.

Lacherra had taught her the quick and dirty method of jabbing vital organs, slashing major blood vessels, or gouging eyes. As part of the gang, they'd taught her to throw fire oil to create a diversion and conceal her exit with a handful of shade's dust, but actual battle with a blade had never been her strong suit.

The crash of cymbals snatched Rosalia back to the present. The world beyond the dressing room had already devolved into chaos, and music thundered from the orchestra. There was a swell in the volume, a rise in the melodic masterpiece put together for their presentation.

Rosalia wasn't meant to take the stage until the climax, when the ugly worm who wished to become a butterfly finally took flight after her transformation. Right now, the other worms were dancing beneath the swaying leaves and grass blades erected for the set design. The heroine writhed in despair, told she could never achieve her dream.

"I love this part," Mira murmured from behind her.

"When the other worms are mocking her?"

"Yes. I love it because soon they'll be proven wrong, and she'll show them she truly is a butterfly after all."

For her role in the show, Mira played the part of a godmother dragonfly, a compassionate but wise mentor to the heroine. As she darted forward and onto the stage, double pairs of wings glistened and left trails of silver sparkles on the air. She circled around the dancer playing the part of the ugly worm and took her hand.

When the worm laid herself down to sleep in her chrysalis, smoke and fog arose from the stage. The theater lights dimmed. It was time for the part of the show the audience always loved the most.

Rosalia hurried beneath the stage and waited until the performer who had played the part of the worm was lowered on a small platform moments later.

"Good luck," Sulie whispered. She'd been painted green from head to toe for the role, decorated with ruby jewels and golden markings.

"Thank you."

They exchanged places on the rising platform, and it carried Rosalia up toward the chrysalis. For her part of the performance, she wore folded butterfly wings attached to her back, mechanical marvels of orange, gold, and black that Frederico had commissioned from some shop in the city. She only had to release the semi-translucent cord binding them.

The music swelled, reaching a dramatic crescendo while viewers held their collective breath, clasped hands to their chests, and watched with eyes wide and anxious.

Magical wisps trailed through the air, the tiny creatures caught on the sand dunes by street urchins Frederico paid to hunt for them after nightfall. Once released, they floated toward the sky like airborne jellyfish, glowing in intermittent pulses of golden and blue light.

Rosalia rose from her crouch and emerged from the chrysalis. It unfurled like a blossoming lily, the pieces of it falling to the side. She stretched and twisted, she twirled and leapt, but her wings remained fastened in place. Flightless.

She threw herself into the dance and became one with the music until the triumphant chime signaled the moment of transformation.

One gesture of her arm above her head drew the cord taut. It snapped. The wings expanded behind her in their full, silken glory, lit by starlight sparkles of glitter and magic. She'd practiced with the things for weeks, enduring many sleepless nights for the sake of the theater.

She jumped and twirled, living and breathing the routine, knowing that, despite a dozen other women performing stunts nearby, she had become the star of the show. All eyes watched her.

Frederico stood nearby out of view of the audience, a proud grin on his handsome and age-weathered face. Beside him, an unfamiliar man watched—a brooding man with dark hair spilling over his shoulders like threads of onyx.

There was something burning in those green eyes of his that sent her heart into an unsteady rhythm. A flush spread throughout her body and tingled down each limb until it reached the tips of her fingers and toes.

Daring to pretend her mysterious spectator was the only member of her audience, Rosalia shimmied a dance of sensual promises and unspoken delights, floating from the stage toward the skyward lights with her arms outstretched and head tilted back. A spotlamp designed to mimic the golden sun bathed her in its radiance, and then the curtain fell.

Chest heaving, she waited until the loft from the enchanted wings lowered her to the ground again. It took two members of the crew to bring her down.

"Bloody things are so light," Mira said as she unstrapped the harness. "Didn't think you'd ever come down this time."

Rosalia grinned. "I didn't either. I was worried for a moment about what the hell I'd do if it carried me to the ceiling. As she shed the enchanted wings, she glanced to her left and saw the dark-haired man hadn't moved from Frederico's side, the two of them engaged in conversation now. Frederico laughed and clapped his companion on the shoulder. Then money was exchanged.

"That's Xavier Bane," Sulie whispered.

"Who?"

Sulie huffed a breath and placed both hands on her hips. "How could you live in this city without knowing the name of the *wealthiest* clockwork mechanic?"

"I don't buy clockwork."

A disgusted sound rattled in the other dancer's

throat. "Anyway, he's rich as sin and just as hot. Look at him. I think he's part elf, maybe. His ears are long."

Rosalia snorted. "There's three or four other races of magical being with tapered ears on this continent. And they're not that long. Besides, that doesn't sound like an elven name to me." Leaning forward, she squinted for a better look at the handsome man. How rich could he be if he brought deliveries in person to his customers?

The girl shrugged. "Maybe he saudoniacized it. Plenty of elves do that once they reach our shores so they can fit in among our people. Take their Ilyrian names and make them fit Saudonia's language to better blend into the kingdom. He built those wings, you know. They say some of the pieces in his store are worth as much as a *thousand* ducats."

An obscene price for a piece of clockwork unless it landscaped the yard, cooked meals, and shoveled behind the horses after supper. With a thousand ducats, Rosalia could fill an armory with high-quality, elfsteel weapons, purchase the freedom of every slave in the city, and have enough gold remaining to commission a crown rivaling the king's jewels.

Rosalia rolled her eyes. "They say a lot of things."

"*And* he's a sorcerer. He disenchants and restores glyphs in damaged magical devices."

"Are you his promoter?" Rosalia demanded, exasperated.

Sulie pressed her lips together and cut her gaze away. "I'm only saying, he's an amazing catch. And he was watching *you*."

"Nonsense. Everyone was watching me."

Mira grinned and joined in. "Everyone was watching the show, but he was studying you like you were a delicious morsel to devour."

They lined up again for the final curtain call, and when it parted, a tremendous applause thundered over the theater. Rosalia bowed low to the ground and stole a glance offstage to the left.

Xavier Bane hadn't moved from his spot next to Frederico. Although the two men were speaking, his gaze remained riveted so firmly upon Rosalia that there could be no doubt she was the subject of their conversation.

3

ROYAL SCHEMES

THE SPYMASTER MOPPED HIS BROW, WITHERING under the stare of King Gregarus Varro XVIII. He alone stood within the immense throne room, all other servants dismissed save for the presence of the king's personal bodyguard. That man, a huge hulking half-giant of a knight, stood nearby. Sir Henric was protector, executioner, and right hand all in one, a loyal dog in elfsteel maille with a battle axe forged by the dwarves of Undercity.

One word from King Gregarus, and his metalclad pet would go into action, deadly weapon swinging, heads flying. The spymaster had seen it once, of course, when the king had declared all members of his deceased father's cabinet to be traitors. Several of his lowest-ranking officers had been called in for a meeting and then summarily executed when they failed to bend knee to the then crown prince.

Swallowing down the nervous knot in his stomach,

the spymaster bided his time, waited for his king's response, and prayed he wasn't next.

Caius was not a brave man, but he knew he only had a chance if he went for Sir Henric first. It'd have to be one hell of a spell to take the knight off his feet and incapacitate him before he hefted the axe.

"What you mean to tell me is that you've wasted both of our time by arriving to inform me of your failure? That you haven't located the device I seek or any information regarding its whereabouts?"

Caius dabbed his brow with a handkerchief. "No, Your Royal Majesty, not at all. What I mean to say is that its current whereabouts remain unknown, but that we've acquired valuable information regarding its theft from the Royal Vault."

King Gregarus stroked his chin. The displeasure and the menace in his eyes faded, dimming to an unimpressed gaze. "Speak on."

Thank the gods.

"Multiple interrogations of your father's remaining advisors and what allies we've discovered have revealed the item was smuggled from the castle years ago and placed in the care of an artisan."

"An artisan," King Gregarus repeated, tone droll. His gaze thinned. "There are a hundred artisans across the city. I gave you specific orders to uncover everything you could about my late father's treachery, and you bring me only guesses and speculation, vague information."

"There are a hundred shops," the spymaster agreed,

"but he mentioned clockwork. I've located only a dozen such businesses licensed to operate within the city."

"And you are unable to determine anything more?"

"Not at this moment, Your Majesty. Advisor Seren held no further mysteries or secrets, and I have absolute confidence that I have extracted all pertinent memories from his mind. Your father never revealed the name of the clockwork mechanic."

"Then we must move forward and discern the identity on our own."

"What will you do, my king? If it's in the possession of a shop in this city, the proprietors have no motivation to reveal this to you. If we abduct a dozen honest mechanics and submit them to my talents, the citizens *will* notice."

King Gregarus shifted on his throne. His gray eyes narrowed into thin slits, nostrils flared. "We can't have that. There must be other ways to ascertain whether our treasure lies within the city walls or has been smuggled beyond Enimura."

"Might I offer you a suggestion? With it, we may eliminate two birds with one stone, Your Kingship."

The king inclined his head. "I am listening."

Flutters of anticipation blossomed in the spymaster's belly. At last, he had the ear of the king and the man's interest. His grudging respect. *Make this good,* he thought. "We must commission the Thieves Guild. There is a practice among those of the Ruby Sands where the desert meets the boundary of the Emerald Plains.

When summer brings spontaneous wild fires, their firemages battle these blazes with pyromancy."

"Yes, I'm familiar with the phrase. Fight fire with fire."

"As this item was stolen and smuggled away by your father and his loyal men, we may have no choice but to involve a thief to steal it back."

4

UNUSUAL CONDITIONS

ROSALIA AND MIRA SHARED A FLAT IN NORTHERN Enimura's Rosewater District, the quarters inhabited by the city's gentry and wealthy folk.

The parlor where they often entertained guests, what few guests they received anyway, was large enough to sit a half dozen people. Among the floor pillows and chaises, they had collected a dozen portraits over the years, most of them landscapes of gardens, the ocean surf, and the plains beyond the desert.

Mira had the better eye for decorating with color. She'd chosen neutral tones for the walls to offset furnishings with upholstery in jewel colors of scarlet, emerald, cobalt, and teal. In each bedroom, separating the bath from the rest of the chamber, they had several standing dividers crafted with soft ashwood frames. The pressed rice paper had been hand-painted with scenes of desert oases and blossoms.

And then there was Rosalia's literature collection.

Mira had little interest in reading, so the three shelves beside the window had been dedicated to a growing collection of works that came into Rosalia's hands. To her credit, most had been purchased, only a few tomes taken while performing jobs for her special clientele.

It was there that Rosalia unwound from a long day of dance rehearsals, evening performances, and nights of theft. She sprawled on a chaise in their sitting parlor with a book in hand, a cup of tea nearby, and the windows open to let in the mild breeze. Living near a bakery was both a blessing and a punishment—amazing for the atmosphere when cinnamon and spices wafted through the air with the rich scent of chocolate, but a curse to her midsection when her self-control faltered.

Mira popped out of her bedroom. "That smells positively sinful." She ran her fingers through her red hair and tousled it while standing in front of a decorative mirror. Among Enimurans, scarlet was an uncommon color and indication of mixed blood with the people of Utopia across the sea.

"Where are you going?"

"Date."

"It's…" Rosalia raised her head and glanced at the grandfather clock. "We haven't even reached the noon chime."

Mira wrinkled her nose. "It's a brunch date. Bonare invited me out for tea and scones."

"Beside us?"

"Of course."

Rosalia rolled her eyes and sprawled into the chaise again. "I bet he tips the server with a clipped copper bit."

"*Rosalia.*"

"He sounds like an obnoxious cheapskate. Who takes their lady to a bakery beside the place where she lives?"

"A man who realizes I love Madame Maxmila's summer rolls and that there isn't a better pastry shop in all of the city, that's who. Make fun of him if you wish, but he knows what I like."

"Fine. I'll give you that."

Mira laced her sandals then drew a scarf around her neck, tugging the edge over her hair. "If you're jealous, I have the perfect solution for you."

"Not jealous."

The corners of her friend's mouth raised in a wry smirk. "Bed a man for once in your life, Rosalia. Or a woman, if you must, but do something to unwind."

Rosalia waved the book at her friend. "I've bedded a man before—many times, mind you—and it was nothing to write home about. Besides, this *is* my idea of relaxation."

"Try something physical and fun and altogether pleasurable. Something exhilarating that'll have your heart pounding."

"I'll do that later."

Mira sighed. "I'm not speaking of second-story work, bitch. Whatever. Do what you want, just try to sound less like a bitter shrew when we're discussing Bonare."

"I wasn't referring to second-story work. I have a

dress fitting with Madame Isabella this afternoon, and I was trying to imply spending money is exciting."

"Oh, that's right. Well, rose is the color of the season. Don't forget that."

Long after Mira left, Rosalia remained unsettled by the accusation. Was she jealous? It would be nice to have a male companion, but she'd yet to find any on her level with similar interests. After all, most of the men of their theatrical group were either taken by equally breath-taking women or interested in their own sex. Hardly eligible.

She'd apologize later. For now, there were books, and the men in the novels she read were *always* available and ideal.

———

ROSALIA CROSSED her arms and stared across the table at her mentor. Her afternoon of respite from the criminal underworld had been interrupted by a runner sent from Hadrian, his excited missive gloating about having acquired the contract of a lifetime.

She should have been at her scheduled fitting with one of the district's finest dressmakers.

"What a peculiar contract. They want me to break into every clockwork shop in the city?"

"They do. Weird and strange request, but it pays well. You're to search the coffers and check the shops from top to bottom for a mirror."

She clutched a hand to her heart. "They're paying us thirty thousand ducats for a damn *mirror*?"

"They've paid half already, love. Whoever they are, they're not screwing around." The elf sat at his table in the vault beneath the Salted Pearl, piles of gold on the scales and more contained in sacks nearby. "Weighed every silver bit and copper pence together with the grandmaster, mind you, because even he couldn't believe this kind of contract had fallen into our laps."

"So what are you doing now?"

"Reweighing it. After One-Hand and I hauled it down here, I wanted to confirm it wasn't some sort of witchcraft or sorcery."

Rosalia moved up to the table and trailed her fingers over the golden coins, each disc cool beneath her touch, their front decorated with the image of the late king, a relief of the palace on its opposite side. Some of the coins, the older ones, still bore the face of Founder Varro. "While I think these are real, the golden shine wouldn't fade for days if they were magical facsimiles. Remember that time Mira brought back a sack of gold from Black Sand Manor?"

Hadrian grimaced at the reminder. "Bloody decoy bags. But no, these would revert by morning. A sorcerer would have to use more energy to bend their will over a mass this large. The more a wizard metamorphs, the thinner the fool's gold spell is stretched."

"Gods. What's it look like, this thirty thousand ducat mirror?"

"The client described it as an oval, semi-transparent

mirror set within a gold frame detailed with five large precious jewels. It'll have a handle."

A semi-transparent mirror? What good was a mirror with an imperfect reflection? "So not even a good mirror since it can't serve its purpose," she muttered.

Hadrian shrugged. "I'm not paid to make sense of eccentric demands. Anyway, I'm dividing the task between you and Mira. You'll hit the Gardens, and she'll search the shops in Gold Valley. Brief her once you have a chance."

"Why didn't you have her called in, too?"

"Tried to. She's occupied." Rosalia raised both brows, but Hadrian shrugged. "Anyway, the enormity of the job requires more than one thief, and you both work well together."

Enimura had the largest merchant quarter in all the kingdom. It was, in fact, so large it had been divided into two districts, wealthier artisans selling their wares from the upper level of the Twilight Gardens, while less prosperous shopkeepers ran their businesses down below in Gold Valley. Locals affectionately called them Uptown and Lowtown, noting the higher a customer ascended, the more money their visit required. It was the difference between seeking fine elven couture and bargain shopping.

Rosalia didn't want to imagine how long it would have taken if she had been tasked to search all the shops alone. "Praise the gods. I thought I'd be hopping in and out of windows all night."

"Smart-ass. Anyway, here's a map of the merchant

quarters. I've marked every merchant who deals in clock-work mechanisms and devices, from the lowliest gear-smith to the wealthiest artisan."

"I doubt it'll be in the possession of the small ones, but I imagine their security will be the most lacking and easier to rule them out."

"Precisely. Be gone with you then. As Mira is assist-ing, she'll receive one quarter portion of the profit if you retrieve it, and vice versa, unless you both locate it and work together toward its recovery."

Those were the usual terms when involving the aid of other thieves. Rosalia nodded and glanced over her shoul-der, itching to go and begin the footwork necessary to case her marks during what remained of daylight. Mira would be pleased to know they were working together. "In which case, we'll split it."

"Naturally."

"Then I'll see you soon." She paused a breath, then added, "I'm not working with her on shit, though."

He chuckled. "Try to return with the mirror. That's all I ask."

Rosalia scoffed. "I'm good, but not that good. You know it won't happen in a day."

By the time Rosalia returned to her flat, Mira's shoes were by the door alongside another pair of larger boots. She frowned. They had a strict rule from their land-mistress—no men inside, a stipulation they'd agreed to three years ago after deciding to share a space.

Rosalia was no prude, but she didn't fancy having to seek a new home, relocate their possessions, or forfeit the sizable deposit they had already paid to Madame LaVerci if the uptight woman voided their rental agreement.

Mira *knew* better. If there was one rule their landlady required them to follow, it was the laws of morality she required all her inhabitants to uphold; no unrelated visitors of the opposite sex were allowed without the proper chaperone.

Up until the day Rosalia ended her scorching hot but ill-fated relationship with her ex, she'd always visited his residence down in Silver Hollow, spending the night in his single bedroom house near the docks. Jeopardizing the home she'd built with Mira had always been out of the question, no matter how many times her sweetheart pleaded to come inside.

Before she could flee and leave the lovebirds to their privacy, the half-dressed pair stumbled into the room still wrapped in each other's arms. Both noticed Rosalia at once, and an awkward stare-off began with her standing in the flat's threshold.

Mira blinked then gathered her dressing gown around her. "Rosalia? I... I thought you had an appointment."

"A runner intercepted me along the way, and I had to see our other boss instead."

Bonare fell back a step and corrected his trousers before donning his mage robes. As far as specimens of masculinity went, Mira's man wasn't bad on the eyes—a handsome enough fellow of native Saudonian blood with the telltale liquid silver eyes of a mageborn human.

He cleared his throat. "You must be the elusive flat-mate. Mira says flattering things about you."

Rosalia bit her tongue, choosing to be civil. "And she speaks highly of you."

He twisted to the left and kissed Mira. "I've got a class to teach. I'll see you later, all right?"

"Of course."

Bonare bowed then flipped up his hood before vanishing out the door in the way that only a skilled magician could do.

Rosalia turned to face her friend once he was gone. "Seriously? What if someone saw him?"

"He came in under the cloak of an invisibility spell." Mira's grin widened like she hadn't been caught risking their home for a five-minute shag. "Let me tell you, girl, his fingers are magical indeed."

"I've heard that invisibility spells aren't that reliable. What if Madame LaVerci had spy eyes or anything else to see through minor illusions?"

"Are you going to make a big deal out of this?"

"You're damned right I am, because half of our deposit belongs to me, and I'm not looking forward to moving with one day's notice. You could have spent two silver bits to rent a room. Is he too cheap for that too?"

Mira's features darkened, and a livid flush spread to the top of her ears, bringing warmth to her entire face. "All because you're jealous. We could have anywhere else with our pick of six other rent-houses, but you chose this one! This one with the silly rules and requirements about guests."

"I'm *not* jealous. They all have stipulations of some kind."

"But none as strict as Madame LaVerci, and you know it. We weren't hurting for the funds when we set out to live away from the rest of the troop."

"You're not being fair."

"Neither are you. He's my boyfriend. I want to be intimate with him in *my* place."

"Mira—"

"So maybe it's time for us to move into different digs. Bonare brought it up at brunch today. When he completed his studies, the academy granted him a private flat in the instructors' suites. I can move in with him, because the mages don't have any rules about gender segregation, marriage, or this other nonsense."

"Fine."

"Fine." Mira turned toward her bedroom door. She lingered a few seconds before calling over her shoulder, "What did Hadrian want?"

Deciding she wasn't bitter or angry enough to keep her friend in suspense, Rosalia sighed and set Mira's map on the table. "He wants me to debrief you about our next job, and he wants us started on it as soon as possible. Thirty thousand ducats soon as possible."

Mira's eyes flew open wide. "Thirty thousand?"

"Yeah. Item retrieval with some strange conditions."

After Rosalia relayed the terms of the contract, Mira bathed and dressed to hit the streets with her. They separated in the markets.

Being a thief required as much homework and study

as it did fast fingers work and stealth. During the day, a wise burglar cased their would-be victims and learned the lay of the shops down to each doorway, blind spot, and window. They memorized the alleys, routes of escape, and the patrol schedule of the city guards.

Hadrian said he wanted results as soon as possible, but the truth of the matter was that it would be a few days at the very least until they could visit dealers with heavy security. The artisans in Uptown were the ones likely to use mechanical traps, pitfalls, and security alarms. They could afford the cost to maintain the most elaborate systems, often designing the bloody things themselves.

A good thief-deterrent system ran about a hundred ducats or more, far beyond what a Lowtown shopkeep could afford. They were lucky to have hounds guarding their shops, though some of the common merchants kept dune kites—enormous predatory birds with talons longer than human fingers. They roosted inside shops and hurled their thirty-pound bodies at anything out of place.

Machines were worse. Birds and dogs could be tricked with magic or handled with tainted treats, but the traps were another matter. Those were things of mechanical beauty, unable to be reasoned with or bribed like a guard. They spewed fire or sprayed acid in precise lines. They clamped down on thief hands and held them secure while blasting alarms until the authorities arrived.

Rosalia shuddered. Ol' Tomli One-Hand had run afoul of a wicked clockwork trap and become a cautionary tale for all other thieves in their gang. Because of him, everyone knew to never rush when dealing with clockwork mechanics who were especially inclined to create their own devices.

Mira met Rosalia at midnight in the lower gardens to compare notes, joining her on a stone bench beside a fountain filled with desert lilies. At that hour, only a few late cordial houses and entertainment venues remained open in the Twilight Gardens.

A cool, floral mist kissed Rosalia's cheeks each time she turned her head toward the gentle spray. "That was enlightening."

"What did you learn?"

"That Master Benicio owns a pair of dune kites and that his apprentice sleeps above the shop. He was too busy wanking to notice me in the store. You?"

Rosalia snickered. "I learned there are many novice gearcrafters claiming to be masters. I also discovered Master Grigio has a mistress who lives in Opal Park. He closes shop early whenever she visits, and they shag in the stock room."

"And when does she visit?"

"Endsday normally, according to the street urchins I questioned. His wife plays cards on those evenings with her friends at a lady's club."

The next day, they repeated their information-gathering efforts. On the third, Hadrian wanted to know their progress, cornering Rosalia when she visited the Pearl to work with Jabari on his lock picking.

"Good work can't be rushed," Rosalia teased Hadrian over a glass of wine in his office. "You know that better than anyone, our most ancient and wizened leader. I thought elves were the patient ones, your lives ever so long and days mere breaths of time compared to our painfully brief existences."

Hadrian laughed quietly and dropped his shoulders. He let his head roll forward and closed his eyes. "You have me there, little one. This elf may be patient, but our client happens to be a very, very restless man, I'll have you know, and as an eager man of such importance, my failure to report frequent status updates has made him irritable."

"Then tell them we plan to eliminate many of the shops tonight from the list, and when we know more, we'll be happy to report in."

———

WHILE ROSALIA EXCELLED at open-hours burglary, what she did best was second-story work after dark. She and Mira had ruled out at least two of the shops in Lowtown and three more in Uptown before taking a break to recover their wits.

Mira joined her on a bench at the square, both of them having donned jewel-toned dresses over their thief's leathers. Modest garments proved to be the ideal disguises when they weren't actively moving in and out of windows.

To the passerby, they were nothing more than two young women enjoying a quiet chat by the flower garden.

"You be careful in Master Nicodemus's shop," Mira

warned. "They claim he has a jlaan."

"I have a flask of fire whiskey in my bag." The enormous, fire-breathing sand snakes reacted poorly to alcohol, a splash of it repelling the beasts and blinding them to both sight and scent for hours. If they were in the process of expelling fire, it mixed with lethal results for the animal.

"Ah, you planned ahead."

"You know it. Tomorrow, I'll visit the Clockwork Emporium. There are only a few other places it could be if Nicodemus doesn't have what we need. I've already scouted out the exterior of the shop. Bane keeps a lot of magical wards and tricks that shouldn't be impossible to bypass."

"I'll be visiting the Mecha Bandit tomorrow. Unless you need any help, I'm retiring from duty for the night."

Rosalia shook her head. "No. Feel free to leave. I can handle this on my own."

Mira nodded and rose from her seat on the bench. "By tomorrow night, I hope one of us knows the location to a thirty-thousand-ducat gold mirror."

They parted ways, Mira to home and Rosalia to visit her final shopkeeper of the evening. Master Nicodemus was an elderly artisan who lived alone, a popular manufacturer of clockwork animals who crafted everything from horses to dogs and birds.

If the item wasn't with him, that left only one other viable option in Uptown.

Xavier Bane would have to be the keeper of the mirror.

5

SOULFIRE

A HUNDRED TINY PIECES OF METAL AND GEMSTONE lay strewn over a black piece of velvet. Xavier spent his lunch break bent above them with a jeweler's loupe in his left eye and a tool in each hand. As one of the only clockwork mechanics in the city trained to alter enchantments with magic, his shop often remained busy from open to close.

But he loved it, and he thrived when panicked customers rushed in with their malfunctioning jewel boxes and timepieces. For buyers requiring work on immobile lockboxes and vault doors, he made home visits by appointment only.

The clocktower at the center of the Twilight Gardens tolled noon, signaling the end of his break. Blast. Once again, he'd let the time get away from him. The bowl of soup beside him had long gone cold, as had the cup of tea purchased with it.

When he gestured with a hand toward the storefront,

a spark of magic flipped the sign from "Out to Lunch" to "Open" and the door unlocked.

Despite the incomparable satisfaction of running a successful business, moments came when he longed for freedom. Long hours whittled away at time he could have spent reading, studying, or creating personal art, and those peaceful but infrequent days of silence became days he coveted.

Xavier was long overdue for a vacation to decompress —perhaps a visit to some faraway place. Maybe he'd travel for a while, and make his way by boat to a distant land. He would even purchase a quality ticket and soak up the sun while lounging on the deck. No steerage this time, as he'd finally come to appreciate his riches and the finer ways of how to spend them.

Humans had the right idea about enjoying the wealth they'd earned, even if some of them took it to extremes.

The bell above the door jingled, shattering his daydream and alerting him to a new arrival. His attention snapped to the young woman hesitating to approach the counter. She stood in the middle of the aisle between shelves of clockwork devices, bearing the regal stature of a princess. She wore her dark hair loose beneath a plum-and-gold scarf, matched by a tunic and breezy, semi-translucent skirts.

The dancer. The dancer who bore an uncanny like-ness to someone he once knew. An ethereal breeze drifted around her like a magical caress. Although he'd never met a *half*-djinn before, he'd recognized her on sight during the performance. The golden aura swirling in the center of her soul danced and flickered like smoke-less flames.

Just like Dahlia. There'd been no human blood in his old acquaintance, but she'd shone like gold. Gods above, he'd wanted her, but her heart had belonged to another man already, and Xavier had only been a cub himself. Could this girl be her child?

Xavier straightened and leaned forward. "Hello. Welcome to the Clockwork Emporium. What can I do to be of service to you?" Besides lifting her onto the edge of his shop counter and putting his head beneath her skirts?

The woman's brown gaze drifted over the store. "I..." When her attention reached Xavier, she stared. Her mouth fell open, lips half parted.

From the first moment of eye contact, he knew something magical had happened, and worried she could see through to his soul as clearly as he saw hers. Did she see the dragon inside him eager to break free of his weaker body?

She shook off whatever spell she'd fallen under. "I only wanted to look around. Is that okay?"

Xavier cleared his throat. "Of course. Feel free to look for as long as you like."

He returned to the pieces of machinery strewn over the soft cloth but continued to observe her with the occasional glance. Numerous carpets spread over the stone floors muted her footsteps—or were her steps naturally silent, a boon granted by her magical nature? He wondered and found he was staring at her again as he had a few nights prior.

Frederico had laughed at him then and asked if Xavier was smitten by one of his star dancers. According to the troop leader, she was one of his best up-and-coming performers.

"I'm told she's quite single and unattached," Frederico had even suggested, nudging him with an elbow.

"I'm not in the market for a wife."

"So you claim, but your eyes tell another story, my friend."

"And what story is that?"

"That you tire of dedicating every waking moment to your craft and desire a companion, of course. I can think of no one finer than Rosalia."

Rosalia. That was her name. The memory came back to him as a cool breeze through the open shop window carried her scent to him. Flowers, smoke, sea salt, and desert sand—three of the aforementioned smells belonged to her, part of her soul, imprinted on her skin, and part of her very being.

The dragon inside him growled and nudged his thoughts, stirring desire and urging him to act.

No. Can't.

After all, women of Enimura had a bias against strange men grabbing them.

Actually, all women had a bias against strange men grabbing them.

Dissatisfied with his failure to act, the inner beast simmered beneath the surface of his human body. The creature standing before Rosalia now was both Xavier and not Xavier, a suit. A costume. Moments like this made him feel like a dragon masquerading as a man, though they were two halves of a whole, always fighting for dominance over the other aspect. Looking at Rosalia, however, definitely made him feel more man than beast.

Rosalia paused by the hanging wall clocks with the exposed gears and tiny, mechanical birds designed to sing a different melody at the start of each hour.

At precisely noon—the city clock tower tolled two minutes early, a fact which bothered him to no end which led him to write city hall twice over the matter—the small doors popped open and the gilded clockwork canary bounced out upon her perch. She trilled twelve lovely notes and returned to her home, leaving the girl mystified. She stared and clutched her coin purse.

"This is beautiful." A price card hung from a thin cord dangling from the edge of the clock. She raised it, saw the price, and her face fell.

And he'd never wanted more to give away one of his inventions for free.

Cool it, his inner voice of reason warned. The human side of him begged caution. It wasn't like him to lose it over a pretty face, but then again, he'd also never met another magical creature inside of Enimura. The standard fare of humans, elven dignitaries, and occasional half-elven servant made up the city's population.

Her soul burned like fire, all the explanation he needed for why he'd become enraptured by her. Meanwhile, Xavier's draconic half urged him to do a number of wicked things to her body, and indecision warred within him, his cock awakening after close to a decade of voluntary celibacy.

Choosing to behave like a gentleman instead of scaring her off, he tamped down his desire and focused on her gorgeous face instead. He didn't like the expression there.

Following gut instinct, Xavier blurted out, "That card isn't correct. It's been reduced to clear and make room for future stock."

The light returned to her eyes again. "Really?"

He grinned. "Really. I have a bad habit of building more creations than I have space to display, and that marvel has been on the shelf far too long."

After setting down his tools, Xavier folded the velvet over his work to protect it. He crossed from behind the store counter and moved beside her. Her smell reminded him of wild and exotic scents found only in the most fragrant desert oasis. Floral and spicy at once, a hint of cinnamon lingered on her hair with the smoky essence of her djinn ancestors.

"How much?" she asked.

"Twenty ducats will do."

Her dark brows raised. "Only twenty ducats? That's a *deep* discount."

He shook his head. "If it didn't sell, I'd planned to disassemble it to create something new. Most people are discouraged once they find out the bird isn't actual gold."

"It isn't?" Her smile didn't fade, and the twinkle in her eyes remained undimmed. She didn't care.

"It's solarite." He lifted the clock from the wall and

took it to the window. Winding the clock back to noon allowed the canary to pop out again, but with the sunbeams shining over it, the bird lit with an inner glow as if it contained its own light source.

Her eyes widened. "It's like magic."

"It is," he agreed. "It's actually a magical component used to augment the potency of spells."

"I thought for sure it was gold because of how it shined..." She sighed.

"All that glitters isn't gold. It's a common misconception among many of my customers when they come into the store." He shrugged it off and took the clock to an empty space on the counter. "If you don't mind waiting a day, there's some adjustments I'd like to make to the mechanics. You can return tomorrow, or I can deliver it."

He could have made the adjustment in five minutes and had the thief-deterrent system out in less. But he wanted an excuse to see her again, a reason to cross paths one more time.

"Sure. I, um..." She nibbled her lower lip. "I'll come back tomorrow."

"Great. What's your name?" Xavier asked, despite discovering it at the theater. He took out a card, dipped a pen into the inkwell, and glanced up at her.

She smiled back. "Rosalia. My name is Rosalia."

"Come back for your clock tomorrow, Rosalia."

"Thank you."

He should have charged her a hundred ducats for the intricate piece, its mechanics and enchantments too complex for anything less.

But damn if her smile wasn't worth every copper of the profit he'd sacrificed.

And in less than ten seconds, she'd be out the door and he'd have to wait another day to bask in her presence. "Wait a moment."

"Yes?" She glanced over a shoulder at him, curious eyes framed by dark lashes.

"Do you have plans this evening?"

The corners of her delectable mouth raised into a slight smile. "No, I do not."

"Would you like to make some?"

———

Rosalia's heart pounded the entire walk home, and for the first time, it wasn't because she'd had a brush with the law.

Xavier Bane had to be the most attractive and charming man in the city. Every time he'd smiled, she'd felt it right in the center of her chest, like a hammer and chisel driving it home until she couldn't see anything beyond his handsome grin.

The skip in her step and the elation dimmed when she remembered the purpose of her stroll into the Clockwork Emporium. After all, she hadn't entered with the intention of paying for anything. She'd gone there to get a feel for his security. Of all the clockwork shops she'd visited, his appeared to be the only one capable of harboring a supposed relic.

She'd broken into several and checked them from top

to bottom. Of the many she'd burglarized, his was the final shop. All roads led to his store, and failure meant reporting an incomplete job to Hadrian. After he'd called her his best thief, she couldn't bear the thought of disappointing him.

At least she'd have a pretty clock out of the deal, if she could never bear to gaze at Xavier's smiling face again after robbing him.

6

LUCK AND SERENDIPITY

MIRA'S INCREDULOUS FACE STARED AT ROSALIA FROM across the sitting room. She worked at a table near the corner, bent over a charmed whetstone while sharpening her favorite enchanted stiletto. Bonare had gifted it to her a year ago for her birthday. Since such tools required frequent care to renew the magic imbued in the blade, Mira had made him teach her how to perform the upkeep soon after. "You've been asked to dinner by Xavier Bane?"

"Today when I went to case his shop, I made a purchase and... he asked if I would see him later. For dinner, that is."

"You're not joking?"

"No. I'm not joking. And I don't have a bloody damned thing to wear."

Rosalia hadn't enjoyed a fancy dinner with a man in three years, not since Adriano was promoted in the King's Navy and wanted to celebrate a return from his first successful voyage as an officer. There had been no more dinners or romantic nights after that. Not really. The man lived, breathed, and would die the naval life.

Mira set the dagger aside and rose, expression grave, as if she'd been asked to rob the city's bank vault instead of assisting her friend with makeup and wardrobe for a night on the town. "Then you need my help."

"Please!"

"All right, all right. I already said I'd help you. Are you still going to complete your investigation of the Gardens tonight?"

Rosalia rolled her eyes. "Yes. For the love of the gods, we have lives outside of our work."

Mira raised a brow. "Says the overachiever who is always stealing, always nicking things if they're not nailed down. *You* have a life outside of work?"

Bristling with mild irritation, and a little embarrassment, Rosalia stormed by her. "Maybe it's damned time for me to get one. Maybe I spend far too much time making a name for myself and taking contracts from Hadrian instead of living as I should. I've had a dozen or more suitors approach me at the theater, but this is the first time I've been intrigued in return."

"Because no man is ever good enough for you," Mira spat out. "Even Adriano wasn't enough, and he's a decorated officer."

Rosalia whirled. For a moment, she could only stare. How long had her friend been holding *that* in? "You're one to talk. You have a senior mage! You didn't settle for a sailor, fisherman, or even a merchant with nothing in common with you. You reached for the stars and found a man who is absolutely perfect for *you* in every way, a man who supports what you love and does whatever he can to help you. For the love of the gods, Adriano wants me to become a simple little wife waiting for him to return ashore—Bonare makes you gadgets to steal with!" In hindsight, looking back at Mira's assortment of gear, Rosalia decided he wasn't such a cheap ass after all.

And maybe she did envy Mira just a little.

Determined to style her own hair and prepare for her evening out, Rosalia strode to her room and sat at the vanity table. After dragging the brush through her hair a few times, Mira appeared and pried it from her white-knuckled grip to take over.

"I'm sorry. I shouldn't have poked fun at you." Mira worried her lower lip between her teeth before adding, "It was more than that. Mean and spiteful is more like it. I know how you feel about dating anyone since Adriano. I can't blame you for having high standards, and you're right. I *am* a hypocrite."

"You are," Rosalia murmured. "And I was an ass for overreacting a few days ago when Bonare came home with you. If Madame LaVerci wanted us out, we'd have found another home."

"A better one," Mira agreed, a grin finally surfacing on her face again. "It isn't as if we can't afford it, right?"

"Right." A few moments passed before Rosalia's rapid heartrate slowed down. "Does this mean you're no longer moving in with Bonare?"

"You know how some of the nobles have a summer home and a winter estate?"

"Yeah?"

An impish smile came to Mira's face. "I'm considering the same. Bonare's schedule is bound to be hell this winter since he's taken on a big class of the younger students."

"How young are we talking?"

"Fledgling mages. Most of them no older than six or seven. He says it's a tough time for a little sorcerer since they're throwing fiery tantrums at mum and dad at this point. Since he's a new instructor, they're his responsibility on top of his current students."

Rosalia winced.

"That's how he feels about it, but he's excited, too. He says teaching a child is rewarding in its own way. Now, enough about us. Tell me how you'd like your hair to be styled. I have a thousand dresses in that cramped closet, and with a little work, we can make one fit."

Rosalia glanced up at her friend's reflection and grinned. "Mira, it's only cramped because you have a thousand dresses."

"All the better to be prepared for when you nick one from me."

───────

WARY OF FLAUNTING a gentleman caller in Madame LaVerci's face, Rosalia took a lesson from Bonare and Mira by meeting Xavier at the bakery instead of the boarding house's stoop where the nosy landmistress would see him. She would no doubt come out to cluck around like a nosy hen.

Prudence also bid her not to share the location of her home with a man she'd only met that day.

After all, what *did* she know about Xavier aside from his fascination with clockwork, his unmatched talent, and the way his emerald eyes sparkled like the ocean water at midday?

Mira had dressed her in the color of the season, a deep and dusky rose that bled to purple near her ankles. Her hair had been arranged in another autumn fashion of many interwoven small braids circling her crown. Those had been secured with gold pearls and shell combs carved from the giant, ebony mollusks harvested off the shore.

When Rosalia arrived, she found her date seated at a quiet table outside, the sun glittering against his hair, and a casual smile on a face so breathtakingly beautiful she thought the goddess of glory had personally sculpted him from clay and breathed the life into him.

"Hello," he greeted her in his smooth voice, rich and decadent, like auditory velvet caressing her hearing with sensuality and unspoken promises. Her knees trembled a little. It wasn't fair for one man to affect her so deeply, so profoundly in only the second meeting between them, and she had to wonder if there was something amiss. "I thought we could begin the evening with tea before touring the Garden district and heading to Saffron for dinner."

Saffron? Rosalia's mouth dropped open. Only the most noble, wealthiest citizens of Enimura dined at Saffron. Of course, getting a table at the elite restaurant required more than money. One also needed to be connected, otherwise the waiting list required reserving as much as six months in advance.

Gods. The man had connections to get into Saffron in the *same* day.

"Rosalia?"

"Hello, and sure, that's fine. Saffron? Really?"

The corner of his mouth raised. "I repaired the oven three months ago during a busy night."

"Oh." Intuition told her the owner of Saffron wasn't the only person of value in Xavier's pocket. The man must have had friends across the city among the rich and powerful. "I hope I didn't leave you waiting for long."

She offered her hand. Xavier accepted and dipped down, brushing his lips against her knuckles. When he straightened and smiled, the warmth touched his eyes and made them come alive with genuine pleasure.

"Not at all. I arrived early and brought a book to keep me company in the meantime." He tapped his fingers over the cover of a leatherback tome on the table beside his cup of tea. A russet stoneware kettle rested over a heating tile in the middle of their table for two.

Rosalia leaned over the table for a look at the spine. "What book is that?"

"*Luck and Serendipity.*"

"An unusual choice for a mechanic," she teased,

familiar with the work of romance from her own bookshelf.

He grinned. "Did you think I was only capable of reading spell manuals and clockwork journals?"

"It's a love story. Most men, at least the ones in my current acquaintance, aren't fond of reading any story where romance takes precedence over the rest of the plot." She pursed her lips and thought of Adriano.

"Your employer seems to believe differently." He cocked a brow. "Frederico writes romantic comedies."

"Frederico is a rare exception. I also have a childhood friend who says romance is uneducated trash intended for women."

"Then allow me to be the first man to tell you the fellows previously in your acquaintance are lacking in quality. Many of the greatest novels of the era are so-called 'love stories' combining romantic elements and suspense with adventure. If a man is threatened by a little affection between characters, perhaps the greater question he should ask himself is why it makes him uncomfortable to read about two people in love."

His answer startled her. She blinked at him across the table, hand frozen beside the tea kettle handle.

"Apologies," he said after a moment. "I tend to be outspoken—"

"No, it's fine. I like it," she assured him in a rush. "I'll be sure to relay your words next time we cross paths, and with *great* pleasure."

They shared tea and spoke for a while at the table, discussing their favorite books until the kettle emptied.

When it did, Xavier placed a small stack of silver coins beside his empty mug. A casual wrist flick summoned an ethereal glow around his hand, and then the book was gone.

He rose and offered his arm to her. "Shall we?"

Rosalia joined him and took it gratefully.

There was something intoxicating about his scent, like smoke, heady spices, and wood. Hoping to be discreet, she turned her head and breathed in his rich cologne, letting the smell of him seduce her senses.

It wasn't fair.

Educated, wise, handsome, and successful, all things she'd always told herself she was shallow to desire in a companion.

Yet Xavier possessed every favorable trait she could want and more.

Until that moment, she'd never encountered a true moment of morality before in her line of work, and now she was faced with the dilemma of failing to complete her mission or betraying Xavier's trust. Only a shrew could enjoy his company in the evening and rob him after nightfall.

I can't do it tonight.

What Mira didn't know, wouldn't hurt her. If Rosalia didn't want to lose street cred, if she didn't want her friend to think she'd gotten soft, she'd just have to pretend she'd enjoyed all the generosity of Xavier's wallet before sneaking into his home and taking even more behind his back.

Besides, he probably didn't even have the mirror.

———

Rosalia made an incredible dining companion, animated and conversational, albeit a little humble when he discussed her talent on the stage and the way her dancing had moved him.

Modesty wasn't a trait among many women in Enimura's gentry, and while she was an actress, not some wealthy merchant's daughter or lesser noble, he'd still expected some manner of bragging. She hadn't.

Following dinner and a little wine, he'd asked her to accompany him for a stroll through the upper oasis where the district connected with Vermeil Hill.

She leaned beside a verdant bush teeming with enormous white blossoms and perfumed centers. "I've never taken the time to walk around the city like this, especially the Gardens."

"Most people don't realize there's more to the Gardens and Vermeil. They rush without stopping to appreciate their surroundings or the beauty of the moon lilies once they're in bloom. This is the finest season for them," Xavier said.

Rosalia leaned down to inhale the aroma wafting from the evening blossoms. They only opened at sunset, the first petals parting when the sun met the horizon. "They smell wonderful."

Xavier removed one of the flowers and tucked it behind her ear. Her smile damn near ended him right then, bursting through his weakening restraint with the force of a sledgehammer until all he wanted was to drop to his knees and propose marriage.

Cool it, Xavier told himself. Not only was it too early, but he was bound to petrify the poor woman and send her fleeing for safety from the eccentric mechanic. His heart didn't heed the warning though. It just slammed against his ribs.

Rosalia had a smile that could brighten the night sky. It also didn't help that all he could imagine at that moment was how much he wanted those gorgeous lips wrapped around a specific part of his anatomy.

The last time he'd taken woman to bed, it had been fruitless and unsatisfying, following the whims of his physical needs without the emotional connection his soul desired. He needed more.

He needed *her*, and while he barely knew anything about Rosalia, aside from the radiance of her smile, he was willing to wait and discover more.

"I suppose this is where we part ways," Rosalia said, her gentle words dragging him back to the present. "A dancer needs her rest if she's to attend practices and perform as expected."

He'd been dreading that. Curious, he popped open his pocket watch and grimaced at the time. It was well after the tenth hour. Had he been courting a woman of nobility, her chaperone would have long ago dragged the young miss away. "Ah, yes. It has grown rather late."

Shyness came over her again. Her gaze dipped down. "Thank you for tonight. I had a very enjoyable time."

"I should walk you home. It's late, and the streets aren't always safe."

Her gentle laughter was as melodic as tinkling bells. "I live in a nearby district, Xavier, and there's a watchman on every corner. I'll be safe."

He stepped forward. "Just the same, I'd prefer if—"

She held him off with a palm against his chest and a smile. "I've wandered these streets at late hours before following a show. I'm a big girl now and able to look out for myself."

Wise enough not to press the matter, Xavier nodded. It was silly to be so possessive and protective of her this early, when they'd only been in acquaintance for a day, but something about her called to the base desires of his animal side. Animal side? Gods, he'd thrust himself between her and danger whether he was in his man or dragon form. "When can I see you again?"

"Um... I'm not certain. I..."

Cutting to the chase, he murmured, "There *will* be a next time, I hope?"

Then that delicious flush spread over her again, warmth creeping over her throat and across the apples of her cheeks. "I'm certain there will be."

"Will you come by to claim your clock on the morrow?"

"I'll try. Tomorrow will be a busy day.. I do want that piece rather badly, though I feel awful for not paying you the price you deserve."

"I'm not worried about the price I deserve. I'll give it to you for nothing if it means you'll smile again as you did this morning." Her eyes widened, so round in her slim face. He dared to cup her chin and stroke her cheek with his thumb, thrilled when she didn't jerk away. "Tell me I have another evening in your company."

"I..."

"Is there another man?"

"No."

His pride wanted—no, demanded—a reasonable and logical explanation behind her hesitation. He had everything to offer her and more, even an escape from the theater if she desired an early retirement. He'd put her on a pedestal and make her a thousand cuckoo clocks in the styles of every kingdom on the continent.

He'd gone long enough without a companion, and for the first time after too many years of struggling through the eternal grind of being on his own, he'd felt like fate had thrown him a gift.

I barely know her.

But he did, didn't he? He knew her soul, and he recognized something in it that transcended common awareness.

He also knew her true nature. As a half-djinn, she could save his species.

"There was another man, but that was ages ago," she finally said. "And it's been a long while since anyone else has courted me—not for their lack of trying."

Xavier lowered both hands to his sides. "Ah, yes. Frederico mentioned you've sent away many suitors."

She shot him a sharp glance, alarm flashing in her eyes then diminishing. "How much has Frederico spoken of me?" A pause, and then she murmured, "How much have you *asked* about me?"

Xavier cleared his throat. "Enough to determine whether to pursue you or not. I was led to believe you were eligible but disinterested in anything but your future as a performer. But when I saw you today in the Emporium, I'd hoped..."

A sly smile surfaced. "Hoped Frederico sent me?"

"Yes."

She glanced away. The white blossom accented her dark hair, and after a day of absorbing sunlight, cast a subtle, silver sheen against the black strands. "Give me a few days. There are some business matters requiring too much of my attention to make plans right now." Her eyes twinkled. "And then we'll talk about that next date."

"All right."

Rosalia stepped back as if that were the end of it, and he considered leaving it at that, letting her go with an uncertain future between them, but impulse drove him forward. He wrapped one arm around her waist and drew her flush against him, crushing a slim, warm body against his harder frame.

Xavier skimmed his lips down her throat and inhaled the scent of fire and magic. It took all his effort not to kiss her right then. He took it as an invitation when she didn't shove him away, both arms raising around him instead.

"I look forward to meeting you again, Rosalia."

She sighed, a quiet breath of approval and pleasure. Her fingers curled against his shoulders, and her head tilted back, baring her throat to him. He was so hungry for her he couldn't help himself and nibbled along the little spot where her pulse quickened. It roared like thunder, loud enough for his shapeshifter hearing to discern.

"Until next time."

When he stepped back, her eyes were hazy with lust and unfocused. He grinned even wider. Fuck yes. He'd made the exact impression he'd wanted to, luring her in and leaving her wanting more. She had become his most wicked temptation.

"Until next time," Rosalia agreed. "Thank you for an enjoyable evening, Xavier." She dipped into a flawless curtsy and headed away beneath the street lamps. He watched until she was out of sight.

Finding her hadn't been a mere luck; it was fate.

7

CURIOSITY KILLED THE CAT BURGLAR

ROSALIA'S CONSCIENCE FORBID HER TO STEAL FROM him mere hours after what had to be the best night of her pitiful dating life. Instead of robbing him, she donned her thief's leathers and moodily traveled the Ghostwalks above the city long after midnight, occasionally casing another merchant's storefront while a pair of her urchins observed Xavier's after-hours routine from the streets and a nearby rooftop. She wasn't heartless enough to spy on him right away.

Over a year ago, calling it quits with Adriano had been easy. They'd had a turbulent on-and-off again relationship, and he'd been besieged by female sailors eager to sink their hooks into an attractive officer. The fates had been against them from the beginning.

It didn't matter that his late mother had been a thief like her, or that they'd practically grown up alongside each other in the Pearl after her mother died. She'd dithered over it for weeks while he was at sea, wondering if it was her chance to leave behind her criminal life and become legitimate. Safe. Cared for.

In the end, she hadn't wanted it to be on Adriano's terms. She didn't want to be cosseted and protected like a doll. Adriano wanted to *change* her into something she could never be. And Xavier Bane would most likely want the same.

But how could she ever know if she didn't give him a chance?

She sighed. So much for the Ghostwalks distracting her from the dilemma of diving headfirst into another relationship. They were both a game and a mode of travel for thieves like her who did second-story work, a pattern of ramps, catwalks, ladders, and narrow ledges that let them navigate the city and disappear from pursuing guardsmen like ghosts.

On a good day of dry weather, they could be a fun distraction and exercise in athleticism. On a wet day, they were death. Suicide. She'd seen thieves try to escape the law on them and slip on a rung or miss a handhold. If the fall didn't kill them, the execution the next morning neatly finished the job. If they weren't members of the Thieves Guild.

Rosalia and Mira had been Initiated during their youth. Others weren't so fortunate, and to become an agent of the Thieves Guild, a small-time burglar had to possess enough natural, raw talent to gain the interest of a sponsor. Without that, the Grandmaster Ombre wouldn't give them the time of day.

Her thoughts seemed to herald the rain, prompting

her to retreat home to the Rosewater District after collecting news from the children observing Xavier. For two evenings, she studied him and learned his habits, outright fibbing to Mira by claiming the man had nothing of importance in his shop, so she'd taken to examining some of the lesser mechanics in the district instead.

If Mira suspected she'd gone soft, she'd have no qualms about entering the Clockwork Emporium and packing her limitless bags with plunder, taking everything that shone from mechanical marvels to expensive tools—even if the mirror wasn't present. She knew her friend, and she knew Mira could be equally crafty at breaking through magical defenses. Lying was the only way to protect him.

I won't steal anything. If he has the mirror, I'll take only that. Only the mirror. Then I can still look into those beautiful green eyes after this without feeling like an asshole.

———

XAVIER EMPLOYED a combination of magical and mechanical securities in his store, some obvious and others not, which meant that the ones in plain sight were intentionally placed to distract from the subtle spells.

She hid in the shadows, crouched on a rooftop adjacent to the two-story building after she'd spied the single occupant of the Clockwork Emporium retiring for bed. He was a creature of habit, extinguishing the lights then heading upstairs. A bit of steam and smoke arose from vent shafts during his nightly bath, and then he appeared in the bedroom where he read for an hour each night.

Darkness then fell, silence. Peace.

He slept with open windows, and one of her spotters, a young boy she paid two silver pieces a night to watch her marks, had reported he remained there until the seventh toll each morning without moving, never stirring or awakening, even when they'd tossed a few rocks against the bricks beside the window.

Xavier was a heavy sleeper, the best kind of mark for a thief like her.

Grinning, Rosalia slid down a drainage pipe to the ground when the guard patrolling the adjacent alley vanished around the corner. Then she scampered up the wall of Xavier's shop with a pair of gloves she'd borrowed from Mira that made scaling vertical surfaces as easy as walking down the street.

I'll have to make friends with Bonare and ask for a pair of my own, she thought.

When she reached the short ledge outside of Xavier's window, she remained crouched there while peering inside. He didn't stir, body motionless beneath the thin blanket. Still.

Perfect.

She raised the window a few inches higher and slipped inside through the gap. Crouched, she stole a glance at the slumbering man in the bed and frowned. Something seemed off. Strange. She studied him for a while longer up close, head tilted until she realized what was amiss.

Why isn't his chest moving? Why isn't he breathing?

Why wasn't there a feeling of life and warmth coming from him, the sensation she felt whenever people were nearby, the way she knew when there were guards on the patrol or her fellow thieves on the prowl?

Her pulse crashed through her veins. Despite all her experience as a thief and instinct telling her to haul ass to safety, she moved closer to inspect the figure in the bed.

Her worst fears had come true and someone had died while she was on the premises robbing them. Or had she entered a setup? Would she descend the stairs to find a dozen armed guards awaiting her arrival, blades at the ready, bows trained on her chest?

Rosalia moved closer, wondering if he was still warm to the touch, or better yet, still able to be resuscitated. She'd recently learned a new medical maneuver brought from another continent, compressions of the ribs meant to restart the heart.

Her hands hovered above his chest, palm down and poised to mimic what she'd seen at the square while the healers gave lessons. Torn between greed for the item and an innate altruistic desire, she chose the latter.

And pressed down on hard wood. Unyielding, firm wood.

It wasn't a euphemism. The man was actually made of wood.

What the hell?

For the first time, she realized something was amiss with Xavier's face. Her eyes finally focused in the dim moonlight and took in features that weren't human. Or elven. Rosalia stared down at glossy cheeks crafted from polished wood, flesh-toned screws visible at the corner of the mouth and jaw. The edge of a wig had been fastened to the brow. It wasn't a person.

The best automaton to ever cross her vision lay in the bed, clothed in linen pajamas with the sheets tucked up to its chest. It had the same shape and dimensions as the man it was modeled after. Marveling over the work of art, she stared at it for a few moments longer before swallowing the hard lump in her throat.

If Xavier wasn't here in bed, where was he?

A smart thief would leave.

A better one would solve the mystery *and* acquire the prize.

Gods. She had to know now. How the hell could she possibly turn back with this kind of juicy mystery looming in front of her face?

Determination flooded through Rosalia, helped by a healthy dose of curiosity. She crept to the open doorway leading into a hall cushioned by a long rug in the style of all textiles imported from the neighboring nation of Nairubia.

This area was unfamiliar territory, a blind spot she hadn't and *couldn't* investigate while casing his store. She held her breath and focused on the silent atmosphere for the buzz of magic, the whistle of spellcraft, or any signs of life down below. Step by step, she descended.

Nothing.

She reached the store counter and surpassed the point of no return. By design, most vaults were dug out of the earth and placed beneath shops, especially the stores of the Twilight Gardens District built into the shelf of the mountain steppe. The rest were usually found to the rear of the shop counter in a secure room. One such room loomed before her, its door hanging open to reveal a workshop stocked with gears, metals, and tools. She ventured there, careful enough to avoid a few subtle spells chiseled into the tile floor. She ducked beneath an obvious trap designed to sense movement and treaded lightly beyond a tricky ward meant to immobilize its victim.

Traps always came in pairs, an obvious one to distract a sloppy thief from the true danger hidden nearby.

Rosalia froze. But a man as smart as Xavier wouldn't stop there. He'd have a third. Something even more insidious if he wanted to punish a burglar. Her gaze darted toward the wall, and she saw it, painted onto the red stones with red ink, a perfect match only visible from the right angle.

Pay attention, she chastised herself. That could have been her death. Or worse. She couldn't determine the type of sinister magic lurking in the enchantment, but looking at it raised the hairs on her arms. The pounding drumbeat of her own pulse became a deafening roar. She waited until it calmed before proceeding forward, scooting to the left, avoiding tricks below, to the sides, and above. So far, only simple magical wards, no pressure plates, and no clockwork beasts or elemental hounds.

Simple.

She crossed the threshold and took in her surroundings. Smooth, moonstone tiles gleamed above her in the ceiling, each one unique and different from the last with miniature craters and textured indentations resembling the heavenly body's surface. A combination wall safe gleamed to her left, not even hidden behind a portrait or some other distraction to veil it.

Whether it was a decoy or trap, it was far too obvious to be real. She ignored it.

Against another wall opposite the entrance to the room, an immaculate worktable lay before her. There were cogs everywhere in bins and hanging on walls, spools of metal wire, tools sorted by size on tables, and so many wonders well worth stealing if she hadn't come for one item and one item alone. She moved about the room with increasing confidence as she became accustomed to spotting his wards, felt the edges of portraits—abandoning that effort when she realized Xavier had better wits than to use the cheapest tricks in the book. She tapped on the walls, listened for hollows beyond them, and finally crouched beneath his desk. He had concealed no buttons, levers, or secret mechanisms she could find.

The vault could be closer to his shop counter.

Where would a brilliant clockwork mechanic hide his most treasured jewels and belongings? He wouldn't use something so simple as a bookshelf door activated by pulling a novel, or a pattern of bricks to tap on the wall. As she rubbed her face in consternation, her gaze darted to the decoy safe.

She moved to it and removed a small alchemical lamp sphere from her pouch. Shaking it stirred the contents and shed light. There was magic there, and it ebbed toward her like a subtle, living force of nature. Her sense of self-preservation told her to leave the safe be. She stepped back from it, shook her head, and then suddenly understood.

Few thieves ever remembered to ever look up. She'd glanced at the ceiling to admire the work, but she hadn't really *seen* what was there. Studying the ceiling revealed an imperfection, one of the tiles reflecting the light brighter than the others. The difference was so minor only the sharpest eyes would see it.

After determining the work table would bear her weight and held no nasty tricks, she climbed onto it and squinted until she noticed a small glyph concealed among the miniature craters in the tile. She touched it and prayed she was right.

Upon contact, a static spark leapt between Rosalia's fingertip and the stone. Somehow, even as the scream rose in her throat, she managed to choke it back and make a pitiful squeaking sound instead.

At that moment, the stone floor soundlessly sank into a deep depression, that revealed the inside of a narrow, descending stairway. Once Rosalia confirmed she hadn't pissed herself in terror, she eased onto the topmost step and felt for magic again. It always came to her as some-thing of a buzz, or a sense of heat or unusual cool where such things didn't belong, magic carrying its own scent in the air, its own taste.

At the bottom of the stairs, she found no further tricks or traps, no floor plates meant to hurl poisoned daggers, no sensors designed to pierce metal spikes through the ground. What she found was something else entirely. The tunnel opened into a receiving room designed to host many guests, outfitted with luxury chairs, velvet divans in remarkable shades of green and teal, and plush arm chairs. The rugs beneath her feet were soft. Silk. Even though there was no one in sight, she moved off their path.

What the hell? She ventured farther inside and breathed in the metallic scent of coin nearby. Lacherra often teased that Rosalia's ability to smell gold was uncanny.

Traveling through several more rooms of increasing luxury, Rosalia came upon the motherlode of all art collections. It lay beyond a wide arch, its space lit by wall sconces powered by magical charms and light emanated by heatless, blue flames. The cobalt glow illuminated paintings and shelves with rows upon rows of books. More rugs in the eclectic and colorful style of Nairubia, their kingdom's western ally, sprawled across an immaculate, polished floor.

There was a feeling in her gut, a pull that told her to continue through the network of tunnels. Left, right, and straight, left again. She'd always called it her thief's intuition, a remarkable sense that told her where to find the most valuable jewels.

The tug guided her through another open archway at the end of a long corridor into a realm of limitless riches.

Wealth beyond anything Rosalia had ever seen in all her life spanned from one side of the vault room to the next. She stared into the glittering space flooded with gold and gasped. Tidy piles of coins rose tall as she stood, and thousands more overflowed from open chests among precious jewels on blankets of velvet.

She'd known Xavier made a healthy living at his craft, but she'd never thought he could have amassed so much money fixing clocks, ovens, vault doors, and airships. There had to be something underhanded and illegal taking place in that store.

And somewhere in the midst of so much wealth, she'd find her answers—and the prize.

Despite her gift, she treaded with caution, too prudent to risk disturbing coins strewn over the ground. She didn't want to alert a potential danger to her presence in the underground lair. He seemed a smart man, and she had no doubt that something had been left behind to dissuade thieves.

Some wealthy members of the city preferred to purchase vault keepers, and three-headed hounds had become a favorite in the recent years. Unfortunately for many owners, a poorly trained hound's loyalty could be bought with a shank of griffin meat. She'd brought some in preparation of this, but exhaled a sigh of relief when she didn't pick out their telltale, smoky odor amidst the scent of precious metal.

The air became too still, the rooms too silent, only the rapid thump of her own heartbeat in her ears. Her palms dampened the inside of her leather gloves, and her mouth became proportionately dry.

Where was it? And why did she feel so much dread?

In the next chamber, the ground had been carved to create four deep valleys with two intersecting paths rising above them. The hollows had been filled with hundreds upon thousands of coins, a king's ransom hidden beneath the shop. More coins than any man could spend in a lifetime invited Rosalia to fill her purse to the brim.

A few unpolished rubies tinkled behind her, sliding down a mountain of gold without any apparent reason for moving. The hairs raised on the back of her neck.

Ignore it. It's nothing. After all, as far as she could tell, no one else occupied the mysterious vault.

At the end of the catwalk, she found several shelves. Books, trinkets, jewels, and an assortment of beautiful, priceless things decorated it. Fascinated, Rosalia ran her fingers over the spine of a book and removed a fine layer of dust.

The Scholar's Truth

A well-loved book written by Saudonia's founder, a wise old man still considered to be the best monarch their kingdom had ever seen. None could compete with his coveted title except for perhaps the late King Gregarus Varro XVII.

And while the man was still a popular figure in history, she couldn't imagine why anyone would keep a book printed a thousand times over on the press, inside a locked vault.

Unless...

Rosalia raised the cover to reveal handwritten ink across the aged pages. She almost died on the spot.

Xavier Bane owned one of the originals. One of seven

famed originals, three lost to time, one in the museum, one buried with the king, one guarded by the church, and one owned by the current ruler, King Gregarus Varro XVIII.

Now it was two lost to time, because she'd discovered one, a fortune that could free her forever from a life of theft. She could sell it to any of their frequent buyers and be on the next boat out of Enimura by dawn. To hell with their client.

It would be a new life for her. At least it would be a new life if she didn't owe Hadrian a fulfilled contract. First she'd find the mirror, then she'd consider selling the book on the open market, growing giddier by the second as she imagined escaping their dusty hell for a world of green grass and verdant forests.

Rosalia raised the book. A gold-framed oval looking glass glittered in the space it left behind.

She rolled her eyes. Of course, the item she'd been hired to steal had to be among the most worthless of everything on the shelf. Compared to *The Scholar's Truth*, the mirror looked trivial and ordinary. She picked up the translucent pane then studied the trio of different metals framing it.

The creator had etched words in an unfamiliar language across the layers of gold, silver, and copper, and the glass portion provided no magnification or adequate reflection. She could barely see herself, and what she did see was distorted and... different. Something told her to look away, so she did.

As she turned her wrist, the glass caught the light of a

nearby alchemical lamp and threw rainbows against the wall. Five coin-sized recesses spaced at an equal distance implied it had once held gems.

Some thief had likely pried them out years ago. She hoped their client didn't accuse her or Hadrian of removing the stones.

"A two for one special," she murmured, satisfied with the night's events.

Rosalia wrapped the mirror in soft leather to protect it and prepared to secure the book as well. Behind her, metal coins chimed again and clinked against each other.

The same cold tickle went down her back, icing her blood and wetting her palms. Fear.

When Rosalia turned, she came face-to-face with an enormous pair of green eyes set above a scaled snout with two slit nostrils. The rest of the head emerged from the coin pile, leading to a slender neck, and broad shoulders. Jewels winked from beneath gilded scales where they had been lodged during the beast's apparent slumber.

Her mouth fell open, and her body froze, knees knocking together.

Xavier did nothing half-assed, and he'd gone leagues beyond having a hellhound or mere traps. He owned the mother of all vault keepers, the kind of monster not even a king could afford—a gold dragon.

The book fell from her listless fingers, toppling to the ground at her feet. She bolted. Dashing full speed down the narrow walking path, Rosalia prayed to every god beneath Enimura's pantheon that she was fast enough to reach the smaller opening before the dragon snapped her up in its jaws.

"Stop! Wait!"

Rosalia recognized Xavier's voice somewhere behind her, but the strange underground acoustics made it thunder around her with tremendous volume.

Keep running. The adrenaline pounding through her veins wouldn't allow her to stop. *Fear* wouldn't allow her to stop, though the underground cavern's corridor suddenly seemed miles long and as large as the city of Enimura itself. The pulse pounded in her ears, but she urged her legs to move until the heart in her chest threatened to burst from its cage.

She'd never make it to the entrance of the hoard in time when every second mattered. Through the open passage ahead, she saw the way in had been sealed, only smooth stone in the place of the open rectangle that admitted her to the vault.

She swore and spun on her heel, glancing left and right until she saw the most unlikely contraption jutting from the wall—a waste chute of the variety often used to carry refuse to the sewers. She lunged toward it and clawed it open, chipping her manicure and tearing the nail bed in the process.

Later, if she survived her escape, she'd wonder why a subterranean vault needed its own trash chute.

Would the outlet support her passing through it? At a glance, she estimated it to be as broad as her shoulders, if not a little wider.

"Wait!"

Keep going.

Death by dragon's maw or death by drowning—one seemed a thousand times more agonizing. With the beast hot on her heels and its owner calling her name, she dove forward into the drain and slid into the gloom below.

8

A MATTER OF LIFE AND DEATH

"And then I dropped the book and ran like my ass was already on fire. I couldn't control my hands. It just happened, my muscles locked up, and I rushed away."

"It's a natural reaction that happens whenever anyone encounters a dragon," Mira explained, laughing. She'd been laughing at Rosalia ever since she climbed through the window into their apartment and flopped onto the floor beneath it, soaking wet and smelling of fetid sewer scum.

Like a true friend, she'd promptly donned gloves, helped Rosalia strip out of the tainted garments, and taken the salvageable pieces to the wash bowl to be scrubbed while her friend stood beneath a hot shower.

Nearly a half hour after her great escape, it was still no laughing matter to her. A soak, fresh leggings, and a clean tunic hadn't improved her mood or returned her pulse to normal. "It isn't funny! I could have been eaten or killed."

"Eaten *or* killed? Don't those things result in the same outcome?"

Rosalia glowered. "Of course. Laugh it up at my expense since you weren't the one running panicked through some madman's underground treasure trove. All those jewels and coins. I'll never see so much money again in all of my life, and I left it because of a damned dragon."

"But you completed the job and you're alive."

"You don't understand. I left behind an original copy of *The Scholar's Truth*." She sighed and dragged a brush through her wet hair. "The words of the gods written as Founder Varro intended. No clever wordplay, no colorful euphemisms added by the temple headmasters. Every-thing transcribed the way the divines spoke it."

Mira chuckled again. "You're my favorite bookworm. Anyway, let's look at the bauble now. I need to see what's worth thirty thousand gold. And later, you'll have to tell me which shop held the bloody thing. I may want to visit."

"Trust me, you don't. For your own safety, I'm not breathing a word. Just... stay away from all of the inven-tors. Hadrian couldn't pay me enough to ever do it again."

"Meh. I run faster than you."

"Dragon's breath is faster than both of us."

Rosalia moved to her pack. Of all her equipment, it was the only thing she'd had to merely run beneath fresh water, the leather satchel completely watertight and saving her belongings from a thorough soak in filthy sewer water. She passed over the disinteresting piece of glass still wrapped in cushioning silk.

Mira unwrapped the mirror and turned it around a few times. She studied the inscription and shrugged. "Oh. Well. Isn't that dull. I expected more of something hidden under the guard of a dragon."

"It was also beneath *The Scholar's Truth*," Rosalia said.

Mira rolled her eyes. "Only you would be excited about a lump of old, dead trees."

After fixing her friend with a disbelieving stare, Rosalia wrapped the glass in silk and cushioned it. "Beautiful, old, dead trees worth more than the sum of all we've stolen this entire year. If you don't mind, I'm going to make sure this gets where it belongs."

"I'll be here. So, erm, where *did* you find the entrance to its lair?"

"Never you mind where. You'll only be eaten."

"Fine." Mira chuckled and moved to a decorative end table. It held a small, stained-glass lamp and a package wrapped in brown paper. "Before I forget, Frederico sent this by messenger for you. He said you'd mentioned wanting it for your next performance."

Mira passed over the wrapped parcel. Within the layers of parchment paper, Rosalia found a small pair of peacock feather earrings. The verdant green, sapphire, and gold glittered as she held them over her palm, attached by golden wires and accented with tiny star rubies.

The price had been beyond anything she could afford for an item she'd wear for a single performance. She blinked a few times. "I said no such thing... I... I saw them in a window as we were crossing from the theater."

"Are you sleeping with him?"

"No! He's old enough to be my grandfather." Rosalia stroked the silky feather filaments and closed her eyes.

No one had ever gifted her anything so precious or beautiful without wanting something in return.

Tomorrow night, she would dance like she'd never danced before, but now, she needed to rush the mirror to Hadrian.

————

HADRIAN EXAMINED THE MIRROR, turning it over in his hands by the candlelight of Lacherra's private office above the Salted Pearl. It was a handsome space, decorated with unique pieces of Nairubian art from her homeland. On one wall, there were feather and bone masks, and on the other, several silk tapestries in dazzling shades of green, gold, and red. A window overlooked the surf at night, a waning crescent moon above the black waters.

His brows squished together. "Is this it?"

"It's a bit dull, isn't it?"

"Certainly fits the description of the trinket. I merely expected... more."

"It's definitely lacking a bit... more-ness to it, all things considered. Thirty-thousand-ducat retrieval fee, dragon vault keeper, and a treasure-filled maze. He could have hidden this in his bedroom." In which case she would have blindly passed it in pursuit of actual treasures. Looking back, she wondered what marvels she'd left uncovered while in his bedroom.

Hadrian grimaced. "Bloody shame you were discovered before you could relieve him of a few jewels for your trouble. Were you recognized?"

"I don't think so. I wore my full thief's leathers and cowl, as well as a hood."

"Good. I'll deliver this at once to our client."

"Promise you won't speak a word of where I found it though."

His fair brows rose. "What's it to you if anyone knows? You escaped a bloody dragon, love. If you can do that, you can accomplish anything, and it's a worthwhile brag."

"I don't want anyone knowing where. You can mention the dragon, just keep his name out of it, please. Don't even mention it to Lacherra. That kind of bounty would tempt even her out of retirement."

Hadrian studied her a moment then dipped his chin in a curt nod. "Fine. Only if you'll get some rest and enjoy your life at the theater for a few days."

"But—"

"No buts. I realize I pressed the both of you unfairly over the past few days, and Lacherra hasn't let a day pass without reminding me that I've been an insufferable arse."

"It's fine. I enjoyed the challenge."

"Were I in any condition to have aided you, I would have." Hadrian kneaded his upper thigh beneath the desk, lips twisted into a deep frown.

He'd joked about at least escaping with the artifact, but the price hadn't outweighed the profit for the ring he'd stolen. A burglar without mobility, was no burglar at all, and while there were other ways to earn a quick coin, they weren't what Hadrian lived for, what the elf had loved with all his heart. He'd been able to scale an eleven-story tower with only a rope, grappling hook, and the nimble agility of the elves.

Now he sat behind a desk, giving orders to others or limping about the city while collecting jobs and odd tasks for them to complete instead.

"You'll heal, Hadrian."

The thin smile didn't reach his eyes. "Yes, of course. Anyway, please, take a few nights to relax among your fellow actors."

"Fine. Put my share in the vault once you collect the remainder." Only a fool would keep that much gold on her person at once, and she could only reasonably deposit so much in the account she'd opened at Enimura's bank.

Impulsively, she leaned across the desk and hugged him. "There isn't a better thiefmaster in all of Enimura, Hadrian. Don't be so hard on yourself. May I ask one thing, though?"

"Shoot."

"Who was our client?"

"That's confidential—"

"A secret for a secret. You know where I found it. Tell me who it's for. Just this once."

He sighed. "King Gregarus."

"You're bullshitting."

"Not at all. So, if you know what's good for you, shut it. Pretend this thing never existed."

"What thing?"

Hadrian smiled.

Downstairs, she found the bar thriving as usual and Lacherra behind it serving drinks to thirsty patrons. Some innkeepers and pub owners out in the city looked down on the dockside bars, claiming their patrons to be undesirable and noisy, but hardworking coin spent as well as money from the social elite. Lacherra made it a habit to always welcome their sailors and dockworkers. Besides, they carried the best gossip.

A small gathering of sailors in naval uniform clustered in the back of the bar with drinks, while a group of dockhands, tanned dark from laboring in the sun, guzzled Lacherra's famous salted ale at the bar and chatted about the recent imports they'd unloaded for the crown.

Lacherra broke away from eavesdropping on them long enough to wave. Rosalia raised a hand in return and debated joining her behind the counter. One glance toward the back of the room ruined that plan, however, because Adriano's hulking form stood out like a flagpole among his drinking partners.

Deciding against lingering behind for a drink or conversation with Lacherra, she cut a line across the crowded floor and hurried toward the door.

"Rosalia!" Adriano's voice resonated, penetrating the din of three dozen or more people. Blast. He'd seen her. She winced and stopped on the spot. "Come have a seat on my lap, sweetheart. It's cold without you."

Hands on her hips, she pivoted on a foot and sent a glare at her old friend and childhood sweetheart. Adriano smiled and exaggerated a pat to his lap, unfazed by her aggressive stare. It never worked on him. "Should I pull the log from the hearth to warm it for you?"

"Ah, you wound me with your cruelty."

Her tense posture eased. "I give you a healthy dose of reality."

"Can't reality wait until I've gotten my hug from you? Been ashore for days now and not even an undeserved 'kiss my arse' from you." She ignored her common sense and moved closer to join the guys at their table. Adriano wrapped a brawny arm around her waist and offered his ale. She waved it off, but squeezed him in return and pecked his cheek. He still smelled like salt. Years of sailing for Saudonia must have infused his skin with the scent of the open sea.

"Too good to drink with me now, love?"

"I've drank with you plenty. I'd just prefer to stay sober the night before a big performance."

"That's right. That overdressed asshole down at the theater keeping you too busy to visit your family here, eh?"

"Far from it. I come and visit Hadrian and Lacherra all the time."

"Why's it I haven't seen you all week then?"

Rosalia extracted herself from his hold. "Because your admiral keeps you under his thumb until sunset." She turned to the others. "How much has he had to drink tonight?"

"Seventh mug is when we lost count," one of the other sailors replied.

"I'm not drunk. Just stating facts. You never come here anymore. Forget the people who helped you back when you was small?"

"What I do in my free time isn't any business of yours, but for the record, Frederico has also helped me as much as Hadrian and Lacherra."

"And my mum."

Rosalia closed her eyes and clenched one fist at her side. "I won't have this conversation with you in public, or while you're inebriated, Adriano."

He rose from his seat, towering above her by several inches. Life in the King's Navy had sculpted his body into a pleasing figure, broad shoulders and muscular arms tanned from days on a ship's deck. "You won't have it with me at any time. Was a time once when you'd be happy to see me, Rosalia."

"I *am* happy to see you. Happy to see you're safe and sound from the patrol. If you want to talk, I'm free tomorrow before the show. I have to go now."

His mug hit the table and sloshed warm ale over the rim. He stepped forward, eager. "I'll walk you."

She pressed her palm against his chest. "No. Unless its a matter of life and death, you can wait until tomorrow."

Displeasure set his mouth into a flat line, blue eyes hard in his tanned face. "Right. Tomorrow then."

He lowered into the chair and reclaimed his ale mug, but his eyes followed her to the door.

———

IT TOOK Xavier minutes to force a shift back to his human body, so overcome by rage he'd thrashed inside the chamber and dislodged several of the beams and marble pillars integral to the support of the cavern. Fearing a collapse, he remained behind in his mortal guise and worked his magic.

An hour later, once the structural damage had been repaired, he threw on his clothes and charged into the upper level of the shop.

It shouldn't have surprised him that she'd penetrated multiple layers of magical wards, swept past the Clockwork Emporium's defenses, and discovered the secret entrance to his lair, given her innate magical abilities, but of all the things for her to take, she'd stolen the most devastatingly powerful and dangerous artifact of all.

The Devil's Eyeglass.

There were at least three dozen gangs currently operating in Enimura at the moment, if not more, and she could have belonged to any one of them. He racked his brain and moved up and down the streets hunting for a remnant of her scent.

And he found none. Good thieves masked their smells using oils manufactured from whale blubber, overpowering their own unique scents while on the job. But something as strong as the scent of a djinn couldn't be hidden for long. It had permeated the disguise, and when she'd run in fear from him, it had filled the treasure room.

He had to find her. If she was working for King Gregarus, she likely had no idea of the danger contained in one little piece of glass. And if it wasn't King Gregarus, the outcome wouldn't be any better, because eventually, the new owner would heed the call from the relic and unlock the magical time bomb's treacherous properties. Sooner or later, late king's prophecy would come to fruition.

Xavier clenched his jaw. He wouldn't allow that to happen. Recovering it on his own was the only solution, finding her before it was either laundered on the black market or passed into someone else's possession.

Think, man, think.

He rushed to the theater. Frederico wasn't as much a friend as an old acquaintance, but if anyone knew where to find her, it'd be him. A heavy rain had swept in from the ocean during the afternoon, obliterating any hope of Xavier crossing an old path traveled by her.

At night in Enimura, the streets were practically vacant, occupied by only the city's criminal element and the occasional roving guard. Most of the latter preferred to remain in the Twilight Gardens, the Rosewater District, Gilded Quarters, and the Opal Park where wealth resided, because they weren't paid to guarantee the safety of the common working class and the laborers who dwelled in the Squals.

Frederico dwelled in a private flat beneath the theater. Xavier had only visited the man's small residence once to fulfill social obligations, but he recalled the door was around the back of the building in an alley, fifteen yards from the service door entrance.

A guard patrolled the street corner opposite the theater, hand on his baton. His alert eyes scanned the street, but he didn't react to Xavier stalking by him, trained to recognize wealth from rabble, even at late hours of the night.

Xavier held his breath anyway and tensed his muscles, a prepared spell tingling on the tips of his fingers. He kept both hands in the pockets of his great coat, hidden but ready to release a harmless sleeping enchantment. He wouldn't kill a city watchman for performing his duties, but he would leave the man asleep beneath a shop awning.

Positive the guard wouldn't stop him, he released the spell and ducked into the alley. At first, he buzzed the bell. Minutes passed, precious minutes, and finally Xavier hammered on it with his fist until Frederico opened the door.

"There had better be a damned good reason for pulling me out of my bed at the second hour of the night."

The words left Xavier in a rush. "I need to know the address of your lead dancer."

Frederico's irritation faded. "That taken with her, are you?"

"It's nothing to do with my attraction to her—"

After rubbing his tired eyes with one hand, the old

man chuckled. "So you admit to being attracted to dear Rosalia?"

Xavier ground his teeth. "It's a matter of life and death, Frederico. Please. I need to know where to find her."

Frederico quieted and studied Xavier in earnest, brown eyes both exhausted and guarded in his weathered face. "For what reason would you need Rosalia at this hour, my friend, if it isn't a matter of the heart?"

"She an item of great importance from me, and I must find her."

"Ah." Frederico's mouth thinned to a tight, displeased line. "I am afraid I'm unable to help you in that matter then."

"Frederico—"

"I can't." And then he had the nerve to shut the door. Xavier reached out and caught it with a palm, overpowering the old man, and stepped inside.

"She's in danger, you old fool. The thing she took has the potential to harm not only her, but anyone who encounters it. For her safety, it must be returned to me. Now from the way you're behaving, the news of her thievery is of no surprise to you. Tell me where I can find her before she or someone else is killed."

"I won't betray her. I'm sorry, Xavier. If you're to discover her whereabouts this night, it won't be from me."

Xavier raked both hands through his dark hair and growled. "Fine." He spun on his heel and strode away, too proud to resort to physical coercion no matter how much the man infuriated him. He'd have to locate her another way, even if it meant scouring every inch of the city.

Two days ago, when Rosalia had swept into his shop, all silk and elegance, he'd never anticipated she would be planning to rob him. She'd brought the smell of the sea with her.

The surfside bars. There were only a few, and he had it on good authority that one was frequently patronized by thieves as a base of operations. There were certain things a man like Xavier picked up when others didn't realize the sensitivity of his hearing.

If Frederico wouldn't tell him where to find Rosalia, if he couldn't be bribed, Xavier would make a counteroffer to her employer to buy the damned thing back.

9

SHELTERED

THE NOTE WAS SIMPLE, A WARNING IN HADRIAN'S neat and tidy scrawl brought to her by one of the urchins shortly after the fifth morning bell.

Take shelter. Bane came here seeking you, and he's furious. I told him nothing and chased him off. Your share is ready. May smuggle you to Clovera for a time until we know his intentions.

Her heart stopped, and sensation in her fingers and toes ceased. Cold swept over her as she imagined the sorcerer appearing at her door with a squad of city guard behind him. But what proof did he have?

Hadrian wouldn't have warned her to go into hiding if Xavier had contacted the authorities to report a theft. The guard would want him to prove it, and even then, they'd be bribed into ignoring the complaint.

How had he recognized her?

Rosalia bolted into Mira's room and shook her awake.

At first, she resisted with a few swats, making grumpy

noises and tugging the blanket over her head until Rosalia tore it away. "For the love of Arcadian, what is it?"

"My cover has been blown. Bane knows I broke into his shop last night, and he's searching for me. Hadrian wants to send me to Clovera."

Irritation bled away, Mira's eyes growing wide and the color fading from her face. "*Bane*? That's who you got it from?"

Rosalia nodded, miserable. Her stomach twisted into a dozen knots, legs barely steady enough to hold her upright. "Now I wish I hadn't."

Her friend tossed the blankets from her legs and slid out of bed onto her feet. "Bonare once told me only the most powerful wizards can control a dragon, and that they're so rare, if the guild knew of one now, they'd bend over backwards to kiss ass and have him as a teacher—as a leader probably."

If Mira wanted to ease her worries, she was doing a piss poor job of it. Rosalia groaned. "Not helping."

"Sorry, love. It's just... controlling a dragon is a whole different level of magical skill."

"Why didn't you say that last night when I came in from fleeing for my life?" Rosalia asked hoarsely, voice barely cooperating.

"I thought you'd know I was joking. I may be greedy, but I'm not foolish enough to go one-on-one with a dragon. What will you do?"

"I'm leaving for the theater. There are armed guards at least, and I can hide out in Frederico's suite until I make a plan. There's nowhere safer in all the city unless I wiggle my way into the royal family. And it's a little too late and a few years past losing my virginity to present myself to the harem committee."

Mira's nose wrinkled. "Ew."

"Yeah, exactly."

"Anyway, do you *know* that he means to cause you harm? What if he only wants his item back?"

"An item I no longer have."

"Point. What do you need me to do to help?"

"Nothing now. Hadrian has my share of the profit, but I won't be able to go to the Salted Pearl to get it."

"Don't worry about the money. Go and dance your ass off. I'll get the gold and bring it to your performance tonight. We'll smuggle you out of the city for a time until we know his intentions."

"*My* performance? Aren't you to be on stage too?"

"My understudy will take my role. I need to pack your belongings."

"Dammit, I don't want to leave."

Mira set her jaw. "But you must. He's a sorcerer, and, if I've learned anything from my relationship with Bonare, they're unmatched when it comes to holding a grudge. You won't be safe here in Enimura, and he won't go to the authorities, because he'll want to handle it himself. Otherwise, he'd have gone to the watch already and reported it instead of seeking you in person."

Cold apprehension sank to the bottom of her stomach and gripped her guts with terror. A few tears welled to her eyes. Hundreds of heists. A thousand burglaries over a lifetime, and she'd never felt crushed between a rock and a hard place before. Was this how her victims felt when they realized their prized possessions were gone forever?

In Xavier, she'd finally met her match, and now a single question remained—would he be so driven by vengeance that he'd track her to the theater?

———

"I'VE HAD the guards escort him from the theater," Frederico announced when he swept into the dressing room. Less than an hour remained before the show, and if not for Frederico, she'd still have a plain face. He'd applied her makeup himself, sympathizing with her anxiety and asking nothing about what she'd done.

When she tried to explain, tried to beg him to let her stay for a few hours after the show, he'd shushed her and said she had a home with him for as long as needed.

Bless this man.

"I can't perform like this, Frederico. I can't."

"You will, and you can. If this is to be your final performance in Enimura for a while, let it be the best and the greatest. Let it be the talk of the city for years to come." He quieted after a moment and fixed her with a long gaze, paternal warmth in the quiet smile on his face. "This thing you took from Bane, it must be quite expensive, wasn't it?"

"The grandmaster kept ten percent. Of the remaining twenty-seven thousand, Hadrian and Mira each took a quarter. The rest is my commission."

Frederico held a hand to his chest. "Gods. Why did you ever waste your time with my theater when you were able to make enough money to buy your own in a single night?"

Rosalia didn't answer at first. She turned her face and glanced at the window, dwindling rays of sunlight turning the stained glass molten with color. "I don't know... I..." She raised both hands and let them fall in her lap again. "I suppose it was nice for a time to pretend to be normal. To be any other girl."

"Then why not let the stealing go? Was it the money? I would have paid you many times more, Rosalia. You are the best. Never tell Mira this, but in my thirty years of theatrical work, I have never watched a girl shine as you do beneath the light. When you dance, you come alive, as if you are a star given flesh and form."

She wet her mouth with a glass of water on her makeup table, suddenly parched. "I enjoy dancing."

"But the theater is not where your heart truly lies."

She considered it. Had she successfully absconded with *The Scholar's Truth* and fenced it, would she have settled in some quiet fishing village with her thousands laundered into bank notes? Would she have created a new identity across the sea, claiming a title of nobility?

Or would she have merely vaulted her riches and continued what she knew best? Rosalia sighed heavily. "No, it isn't."

Her gray-haired friend rubbed his head. "I understand. The Master of Fate teaches us that, does he not?

We each have a true passion, a destiny awaiting us above all other desires."

"If only mine were legal," she muttered bitterly.

"One day, this talent of yours will be useful to you for matters beyond personal gain. You wait." He removed a flask from his belt and pressed it into her hands. "Here. A sip for your nerves."

She unscrewed the top and drank the strong liquor despite her words to Adriano the previous evening. Initially, she grimaced at the taste until it rolled over her tongue and transformed from its natural licorice-flavor, becoming sweeter than ripe cherries. She savored the transformative wine and sighed. The flavor was different for everyone, a true drink to savor. The final notes became a hint of succulent berries and chocolate.

"Now, what shall I tell the other gentleman caller?" Frederico asked.

"Other gentleman caller?"

"Yes. The large one who sometimes visits you."

"Shit. I told Adriano I'd speak to him before the show."

"Should we permit him entrance? He's waited quite patiently."

"Yes."

Frederico squeezed her shoulder and left the room. Minutes later, knuckles rapped against the door, and Adriano's muffled voice reached her. "Rosalia?"

"Come in."

The door opened and shut behind him. He approached without speaking, handsome as ever in his uniform, the pristine white of the king's navy. He wore his sword on his hip and all the ribbons denoting him as an officer.

She'd been so proud of him when the admiral promoted him three years ago, and they'd celebrated the night away, drinking until the sun rose, because he'd had only a few days before it was time to ship out again.

And for a while, their relationship had made sense. She didn't like to be smothered. He was always at sea. But there came a day when she'd wanted more. More had meant a partner who wasn't gone for three or four months at a time, a partner who supported all of her ventures.

"I didn't think you'd let me in," Adriano spoke up first.

"A few unforeseen events happened since we spoke last night."

A deep furrow formed between his brow. "I see. This still a good time to discuss us?"

Us? He said it as if there was something between them besides friendship.

"There hasn't been an us in over a year, Adriano."

"I've been to sea for six months," he gritted out. "A year ago, you asked for space, and I gave it to you, but I hadn't realized it would be the end of our relationship. You loved me once."

"I've never uttered the words love in my life without referring to muffins from Madame Maxmila's bakery." She opened the small package with her peacock feather earrings and slipped them into her earlobes. "We are two different people. You're a man of the military."

"And you're a thief," he said bitterly, spitting it out. "You could give it all up. Is it worth so much heartache? So much strife and danger? Look at what you have here."

A tiny spasm of guilt trembled behind her ribs. Rosalia swallowed and glanced away, breaking eye contact between them. How could she possibly tell her oldest friend, the only person she'd known since her first day in the city as a child, that she was leaving for an undetermined amount of time?

She closed her eyes. "I don't even have this anymore, Adriano. Tonight will be my final performance. Last night, my heist went sideways. I thought all was safe, but he confronted Hadrian. Knows my name. It's only a matter of time before he knows where I live as well."

When she risked a glance up at Adriano, she saw his face had gone ashen. Gray. He stared at her. "Who is he?"

"Xavier Bane."

"The sorcerer mechanic."

"Yes. And we all know the will of sorcerers. I'm safe for now while I'm inside this building, and Frederico has barred him from entering the theater, but it's only a matter of time before these walls become my prison, rather than a shield."

"So, what will you do?" he asked, voice softer.

"Mira and Hadrian are arranging a transport for me to leave the city. I'll be smuggled out. Start a new life elsewhere."

"I'll come with you."

"If you desert the navy, you'll lose everything you've

worked to achieve. You'll be branded a traitor to the crown."

"Rosalia—"

"I won't let you do it. I don't *want* you to do it. This is my mistake and my problem."

Adriano clenched his jaw. "I see. What if I pull a favor or two and arrange for Bane to have a few problems. I have pals in the watch."

"Who will accept bribes as necessary from our wealthy merchant to turn the other way while he murders me. He can't bribe an entire theater, and respect for Frederico seems to keep him at bay for now, but I have no doubt that the moment he catches me unaware, I'll go up like a tinder twig in a bonfire." A wan smile curved her mouth.

Adriano knelt in front of her and took both of her hands. His touch was rough, fingers calloused from years of working aboard ships. An officer's life hadn't changed it. "Don't joke like that."

"If I don't, I'll go mad." Gently, she withdrew her hands. "I have to go on stage soon."

"When will you leave?"

Her teeth skated over her lower lip. "Tonight possibly. Depends on how quickly they can accomplish it."

One of the other girls knocked on the door. "Rosalia? Curtain rises in five."

"I have to go."

Adriano rose and brushed a hand down his pants. "I'll be in the naval officers' box."

"I know." She tilted her face up to him and smiled. "Maybe we'll see each other again someday."

"No maybes about it, sweetheart. We will."

He hugged her, and for a moment, for one blissful and sweet moment, she felt safe in his arms, until she remembered the merciless vengeance of mages and knew Adriano would go to his death for her. Better to leave and spare him that.

10

BURNED

A THUNDEROUS APPLAUSE SPILLED THROUGH THE curtains. It had been the best and most difficult dance of her life, an act of absolute perfection despite fearing she hadn't practiced enough over the days since receiving the job for the mirror.

Adriano had given his word and watched every moment.

Afterward, once she'd taken a bow on the stage and hurried into her dressing room to fret and pace in peace, Frederico knocked.

"Come in."

The older man stepped inside, looking weathered and stressed, his mouth pressed into a joyless line and eyes creased heavily with more crow's feet than she remembered. He held a wrapped bundle in his arms, and she could guess at its contents. Her leathers. "I do not want to give these to you, and I do not want to watch you leave, but I must if you're to be safe."

Rosalia blinked a few times to clear her vision. "Frederico..."

"You are like a daughter to me, Rosalia. There were times I told myself perhaps in another life, you could have been. I swear to you that I will smooth this over with Xavier. Whatever it is, whatever reason you believe you are in danger, I will fix it."

"I don't think it can be fixed."

"I do. Perhaps you should speak with him. He says he only wants to talk. That many people are in danger because of this thing you took from him."

Could it be true? But what danger could there be in a mirror?

"Anyway, consider it. Mira brought these for you." He pushed the parcel into her arms, and the neutralizing scent of whale oil and shade dust wafted off the package. The mixture had its own unique odor, a musky smell of tanned leather and the desert after a rare rainstorm.

"Thank goodness."

"She also said to tell you the preparations are complete."

"What do they want me to do?"

"Dress and wait here for Hadrian to come retrieve you. Mira is packing your belongings and taking them to the smugglers."

Trumpets blew outside. Rosalia peered through the window in time to see guards assembling in the streets and marching toward the south.

Then there were alarms screaming from the north end.

Frederico paced by the door. "Those were the blaze sirens. The fire brigade only sounds the alarms when there's a disaster in the city. Something must have happened."

"Something's definitely amiss."

When an hour passed without sign of her friends, Rosalia made her way into the upper level of the theater and climbed out onto the roof for a look at the city. To the south along the border near the docks, she saw curls of smoke rising toward the darkening sky. Within the next thirty minutes, three more massive fires ignited across the city, and then a patrol of guards swept through the streets. They declared a citywide curfew and banished every civilian to their homes or businesses.

Frederico flagged down a passing runner, but the man shook his head and continued. Messages were closed.

If she wanted to gain any insight into what was happening, she'd have to go out on her own. Making her decision, she finished donning her gear and tossed her cloak around her shoulders. "I'm leaving."

He sighed. "I suspected you would say as much. Perhaps the confusion and the chaos caused by the fires will be enough to protect you this night."

Within minutes of taking to the streets, she discovered most of the noise and commotion from the city watch and royal guard came from the Squals—the poor quarters far beyond the wealthy districts. She kept to the shadows and avoided their notice until she made her way toward the warehouses beside the docks. Those rooftops made an ideal spot to conduct surveillance.

After finding the ideal vantage point, she knelt and removed her scope.

A burning husk was all that remained of the Salted Pearl, two stories of beachside tavern reduced to smoky rubble. She stared at it, an iron fist squeezing her heart.

This can't be right. This can't be real.

Rosalia swept the scope down the beach, desperately seeking the silhouette of Lacherra or Hadrian among the spectators and positive she'd see the former giving some city watchman a piece of her mind for torching her bar.

Instead, she saw the royal guard patrolling the beach in force and the battered body of Ol' One-Hand nearby covered in bloody sword lashes.

No, no, no!

Barrels and crates of their belongings had already been removed to the beach and some dockworkers were loading those onto the confiscation carts. Desperate to understand what had happened, she swept the scope down the beach until she saw the telltale arm stripes of a city watch sergeant and read his lips.

"—bloody thieves den left. Are you certain we've got the leader? Ah, good. The only good elf is a dead one. Make sure nothing remains for any stragglers that—" He turned aside, the rest of his words lost.

It didn't matter. A few heartless words had told Rosalia everything she needed to know about the city watch's recent activities. Grief hit her like a punch to the throat and sent tears flooding down her cheeks, shoulders shuddering and raw sobs escaping her constricted throat. Not Hadrian. If Frederico was a grandfather to her, then Hadrian was the father she'd looked up to and loved with limitless affection, not a leader or a boss.

She wept until she wanted to vomit and her throat ached. Her body shook, and her chest hurt from retching afterward. Wherever she looked, great pillars of dark smoke rose toward the night sky during the city's campaign against the Thieves Guild, more than a dozen dens reduced to rubble in what had to be the single most organized extermination in the city's history. And still, there were many more, because she'd memorized most of their locations over the years with exception to a small handful kept in total secrecy. Would the guard find them as well?

The Sewer Rats were aptly named for their fondness of the city's rocky undercrofts, hidden paths, and sunken roads. They had a lair somewhere down there that was absolutely secret from the rest of the guild, a place no one outside of their gang was allowed to tread.

Rosalia didn't believe much in the power of prayer, but she prayed now for the thieves who made their home in the darkest, dankest tunnels of the city's underground waste system. Most of them were merely children, their leader a few years shy of reaching his teens.

Please, Lady Fortune. Please spare them. If you spare any of us, spare the little ones.

By the time the pain finally lessened enough for Rosalia to move again, the guards had extinguished the flames. She made her way toward the smoldering remnants of the Pearl where a few embers still shone bright against the sand. There was so little left of the tavern, scarcely more than a burnt husk, gutted by fire.

Inside, she found a single unrecognizable body behind the counter with a metal crossbow bolt in her throat, another corpse near the door.

But she knew it was Hadrian. It could be no one else, his favorite watch reduced to a lump of hot metal around one wrist.

There had to be someone left. Had to be someone who had survived the purge of the city's thief network. Desperate to meet a single burglar or bandit, she hurried into the warehouse district again and melted into the shadows. There were paths and alleys the common folk didn't take for fear of attracting Enimura's criminal element, or worse—corrupt watchmen.

———

DESPERATE TO FIND ALLIES, Rosalia hurried into Vermeil Hill for the residence of the notorious loan shark Marcolo Aleppo, a man with so much power he'd dragged even the captain of the city watch into his debt. When the legitimate counting houses declined to give a loan, Aleppo's agents acquired the information and offered sweet deals in his name. And when they failed to meet the terms of the loan, his people gleefully extracted payment in alternate ways—all within the rules of the Thieves Guild, of course. Aleppo liked to have people in

his debt, viewing favors as more valuable currency than
actual gold.

The four-story building occupied a posh section of
Vermeil Hill opposite the district's main fountain square,
flanked by a handful of accountants and finance brokers
bribed to turn down key figures throughout the city for
loans. There was a carriage outside the narrow alley and
several of Aleppo's men were loading trunks inside. Then
she saw the man himself, a figure with broad shoulders
and chiseled features, neatly trimmed dark hair, and
cool eyes.

Desperate to learn anything about the raids, she
rushed from the shadows toward their vehicle, only for
the thundering of horse hooves to come bustling from the
north end of the street. Watchmen. They arrived in
groups of four, filling the streets and wielding crossbows.
Each small group appeared to be led by a member of the
Royal Guard, identified by their flamboyant red capes.

Aleppo's men moved into action with their own
ranged weapons. As bolts flew back and forth, a
swordsman leapt into the fray spinning curved blades as
long as Rosalia's arms in an acrobatic display of martial
prowess. All of his bodyguards, save for the one with the
swords, resembled desert sand giants. They formed a wall
between their boss and his attackers.

Rosalia ducked behind the stone fountain as the battle
wore on. There was nothing she could do to help them—
the loan shark and his people had been outnumbered three
to one by a combination of skilled city watchmen and royal

guards. A bolt struck the carriage driver in the chest, and then the doors were torn open. Marco Aleppo fired a round from his pistol. The ball struck one watchmen in the face, getting lost in his eye socket in a spray of blood. He collapsed and fell back, but two more took his place.

She sucked the breath between her teeth. Those things were outlawed in Enimura, possessed only by military officers and viewed as unstable, unnecessary craft by anyone else. Only a few private collectors were willing to take the risk to purchase them on the black market. It didn't matter. The weapon didn't help him at all since the ever-increasing squad of watchmen swarmed over the carriage. Guards with truncheons overcame the swiftest bodyguard and beat him into the ground. Soon, the swordsman was a motionless shape on the alley floor.

A pair of royal guards neared the fountain, chuckling from astride their horses. "Shall we burn this building?"

"No. We don't want to risk spreading the damage to the rest of Vermeil."

Hoping to find them distracted with their fresh catch, Rosalia searched for an escape route and saw only a narrow path between the jeweler and a tailor. There wasn't a single shadow, lanterns and city lights illuminating the district square. She froze, petrified by the likelihood of joining Aleppo's gang and sharing their fate. The moment she moved, they'd see her, but the alternative of lying in the fetal position beside the fountain until they stumbled over her wasn't any better.

She forced her paralyzed limbs to cooperate and darted out.

"One is getting away!"

"No one escapes! Get them!"

Rosalia ducked to the side, narrowly missing a bolt. It tore through her cloak and pinned it to a wooden post until she ripped it free.

Horse hooves thundered behind her against the cobbled street, and then a tingle of intuition danced across her shoulder blades like the skeletal fingers of death. When she ducked, another bolt missed her by mere inches. It was so close, she heard the whistle of it slicing through the air. It stirred her hood and kissed the edge of the fabric in passing without piercing it.

A desperate running leap threw her onto a short ladder leading to the rooftop.

"Let no one escape!" The royal guard captain's voice bellowed across the dark skies. "I want every last thief dead or in our custody."

His declaration filled her body with dread and dropped a lump of ice in the pit of her stomach she couldn't ignore. While she took the Ghostwalks across the rooftops, a few watchmen broke away and followed her on horseback.

She had to shake them, had to lose them from her trail somehow and take cover at Frederico's place. She feinted left and whipped a sachet of shade's dust from her cloak. It exploded against the street below and created a cloud of black, swirling sands enchanted with the essence of shadow. Rosalia darted right, but she stumbled on the ledge and lost her balance. One moment, there was solid roof beneath her and stone molding. In the next, open air and wind rushed up toward her. She was falling.

As she plunged through the city streets below, her final thoughts were of how much she'd never accomplished, the dances she'd looked forward to performing for Frederico, and the promises she'd never keep to teach Jabari the art of legerdemain.

And how much she regretted failing to leave a certain mage's jeweled mirror alone.

———

XAVIER BARGED into Frederico's apartment. The smell of her was everywhere, flooding his nose and his senses with both the smoky scent of her aura and the blasted coverup she'd used to disguise her smell. Whale's oil and something else, something he couldn't quite place. While it was a good trick, it was also a cheap one, and he wouldn't fall for it again. It neutralized everything about her but that subtle hint of djinni spirit that clung like a tenacious note of jasmine smoke at the end of every deep inhalation.

"I'm finished playing with you both. I need to see the girl at once. Right this moment."

Frederico's personal suite wasn't large, and the open kitchen lay adjacent to the sitting parlor where he entertained guests. The man was wrapped in his dressing gown, standing beside the stove with a coffee mug raised toward his mouth.

To his credit, he didn't spill it. "Many thanks for not shattering the entire door, but she isn't here."

"You may think you're protecting her, or even helping her, but you aren't. She's in danger."

"Funny, but the girl and her associates seem to think you're the true danger, Xavier. Tell me, why should I turn her over to you?"

Xavier strode up to him and set both hands down on the counter. He leaned forward, jaw set and ire rising because he'd had enough of idiots for one night. "Yes, she did take something from me, but at the moment, I'm more concerned with her safety. You know me. I don't care what foolish notions she and that elf have in their heads about mages or revenge. I only want to see her safe, mate. That's it."

"Safe from what? If not you, what danger is there?"

"At the moment? Everyone who receives a wage from the crown. I tried to tell that fool elf, but he didn't heed my warning, and now he's *dead*."

"You killed Hadrian?"

"No!" Xavier raked a hand through his dark hair and growled. "At this very moment, teams of city watchmen and royal guards are combing the city, under orders from the spymaster general to capture all thieves. Those who won't go peacefully are being murdered where they stand."

The color leached from Frederico's face, turning his ruddy skin chalky and pale. "You can't be serious. That's... not merely preposterous, it's impossible! How could they find so many thieves at once?"

"I don't know, but I witnessed enough out there while searching for her to believe they'll have the matter all sewn up before sunrise. The streets are running red with thieves' blood, and she'll be among them."

Frederico sagged against the counter. "She went to the beachside to find Hadrian and Mira. Her gang is located out of the Salted Pearl. That's all I know."

"The city watch razed the Salted Pearl three hours ago, Frederico. There's nothing left."

Grief twisted Frederico's expression into such earnest despair, Xavier had no doubt the man had spoken the truth as he knew it. "Then she's dead. She's gone, isn't she?"

"No. I don't think so... not yet anyway. That girl has the luck of the divines on her side, but everyone's luck runs dry eventually. Where else would she be? You know her better than I do. Where else would she go?"

"She lives in a boarding manor in the Rosewater District. She may have wanted to see if Mira was there. When neither Hadrian nor Mira arrived as promised, she grew worried and ventured out on her own to seek them."

"I see."

"You must find her, Xavier. Please. I'd consider myself forever in your debt if you can bring her home to me. Bring my girl home safe."

"I will."

With Frederico's directions to Rosalia's residence, he broke curfew again and sped down the street under the cover of a minor invisibility charm while watch whistles echoed through the night. He arrived to find the manor in flames and neighborhood residents standing in the streets in varying degrees of undress, most of them clothed in dressing gowns and nightwear, some barefoot and clutching small luggage with what they must have taken before the flames spread throughout the building.

A breathless fellow in only his linen pajama bottoms dashed toward them, out of breath. "I tried... tried to flag down a watchman, but he wouldn't... wouldn't hear it." He gasped in a few thirsty breaths while the eager crowd gathered around him. "They're on the move toward Silver Hollow. Something about thieves."

The oldest woman wailed, her keening cry of despair sharper than a knife. "Thieves? That is what occupies the watch? What of the Mages Guild?"

"A sorcerer at their office in the Twilight Gardens said they'll send a representative soon. I'm sorry, Madam LaVerci. I tried my best."

A middle-aged man paced the cobbled street and wrung his hands together. He wore the season's finest style of tailored linen and squinted through the rising shroud of black smoke, gaze darting from the burning home to the adjacent manor. "They had better arrive soon or we'll all be homeless."

These people don't have time to wait for the damned guild, Xavier thought. He hurried up to them as a growing crowd formed behind them, other inhabitants of the neighborhood gathering to watch the flames. "Excuse me. Excuse me, madam. What happened here?"

The presumed homeowner spun to face him, tears streaming down her wrinkled cheeks. "There was a commotion outside of my home, and then suddenly there was an explosion."

"It rocked the entire manor," the half-dressed runner agreed. "I was having a smoke on the terrace when it happened." He nodded to a home across the street facing the boarding house.

"Did you see anything?" Xavier asked.

"Nothing. It sounded like a scuffle though. I heard a woman scream, and then flames started crawling up the building."

"Do you know if all of your tenants are accounted for?"

"They're not. There are two young ladies, two girls who live on the second floor. I heard someone calling for help from that direction." The woman wiped her face with the heels of her palms. "Why hasn't someone arrived from the Mages Guild yet?"

A young woman stared at the burning home with tears streaming down her cheeks. "There are fires across the city. Those must be more important than our home."

"Fires the city watch has caused!" shouted another man. "A friend of mine in Gold Valley says he watched them set flame to a shop in the middle veranda."

"Setting fires?" Madam LaVerci clutched a liver-spotted hand to her heart. "What in the name of the gods could be more important than our lives to the city watch?"

"Something awful," Xavier murmured. He stared at the building, and then he did the only thing he could do under the circumstances. He shoved up his shirtsleeves and prepared to enter. "Second floor you said? I'll go in after them."

Madam LaVerci reached for his arm, a frantic swipe skimming past his rolled cuff. "You can't, sir. We were lucky to get out with what we were able to grab. It's death for anyone to go in there now."

Another member of the crowd muttered, "Look, he's an elf. Maybe he's a mage. Mages can do all kinds of things with fire, Madame LaVerci."

No. Not a mage. Better than that. He was a dragon, and his natural resistance to fire provided all the encouragement needed.

"Rosalia and Mira live in the west wing of the second floor. Please, young man. Save them if you can."

Xavier raised both hands before him and positioned his fingers in the arcane gestures of a storm summoning. Thunder rolled and a flash of lightning lit behind the dismal, gray clouds that had haunted Enimura for the past two days, and then a light mist shimmered from the sky. He waited a few seconds—precious seconds for the intensifying cool rain to seep through his clothes and slick down his hair—then he charged into the burning building.

The smoke rushed up his nostrils and into his lungs, a mere irritant instead of a lethal hazard. He raised the damp neckline of his tunic above his nose and rushed forward with his left hand before him, channeling energy and forcing the fire to part until he was granted an open path through a home reduced to chaos and ruin. Flames danced across the silk damask walls and spread over the ceiling, great waves of black smoke rising. Heirloom portraits crinkled and blackened. So much beauty gone in seconds.

Please don't be here. Would a half-djinn have the same immunity to fire as her pureblood parent? He hoped so—no, he prayed so. The stairs creaked dangerously beneath his weight, and the flames racing down the bannister length licked his bare arm. Instead of blistering the skin and searing through him, they left a mild, reddened mark. In a few minutes, that would fade as if nothing ever happened. Being a weredragon had its benefits from time to time.

A few yards from the landing, Xavier found the door to the flat shared by the two ladies. Prepared for the worst and armed with a magical shield, he thrust with his power and blew through it. The door splintered into a hundred scorching pieces, and the expected backdraft washed over him, roaring against the defensive spell. His magic held up against the onslaught, though a hairline fissure formed in the semi-translucent barrier.

"Rosalia! Mira!" He called for either woman, and when no one answered, he entered the plane of fire that had become their suite.

The area was open and spacious but filled with flammable objects, everything from the designer rug on the floor to the bookcases teeming with novels ablaze. Flames engulfed the curtains of a closed window. He found a body in the threshold of a bedchamber, burned beyond recognition but too tall to be Rosalia. Had to be Mira. She'd been wearing black leather.

"Rosalia!"

The rear bedroom was inaccessible, but he didn't smell charred flesh arising from what he presumed was Rosalia's living quarters.

If she wasn't there, it meant she was still on the streets.

He just had to find her before the watch did.

11

ALONE

Rosalia lay surrounded by rotten food and filth on an open heap contained in one of the city's many trash wagons. Someone had tossed horse dung inside of it recently to add insult to injury, but since it had broken her fall, she didn't have too many complaints.

Shit could wash off. Broken bones weren't so easily fixed.

While she recovered from the terror of tumbling off a two-story building, she listened to boots rushing past the trash pile and shouts echoing through the night. A pair of them stopped, the watchman winded from the exertion of chasing her on foot.

"Where'd she fucking go?"

"No clue. Blast it all. Could have sworn she'd run this way after trying to trick us."

They'd caught on to that?

She held her breath and waited until there was silence before she dared to crawl off the wagon. She knocked what she could off her, dropping a few rotten apple cores, banana peels, and equine excrement off her cloak before deciding to ditch the garment altogether. She'd buy another. Eventually.

Was it worth heading to the Rosewater District to search for Mira there?

No. Fearing she'd only encounter more guards patrolling the streets, she took an indirect route to the Gilded Quarter and hurried back to the theater hopeful to find Frederico waiting for her. He opened the door at the precise time of her arrival, either blessed with a sixth sense or the divine patience to stare out the window for her. She stumbled forward and collapsed into his arms the moment he shut the door against its splintered frame.

"It's... it's... aw-awful," she gasped between desperate breaths. Her chest hurt from pushing herself, and her back ached from the tumble she'd sustained from the roof, even with trash to cushion her fall.

His palm smoothed a circle over her back. "Shh, shh. Breathe, child. Breathe."

"They killed Hadrian and Lacherra. They killed everyone. Burned the Salted Pearl."

"I know. I know. Gods, I thought the worst. Thought you were dead or captured by now."

How could he possibly know what had happened when he'd been safe and sound inside the Gilded Quarter? With the danger of the streets behind her, the reality of what had happened crashed down against her, cracked open her chest and replaced her heart with blistering cinders.

Desperately wiping her cheeks with her wrist, she followed Frederico's guidance and let him lead her to the enormous divan. He stepped away and returned moments later with a finger of hard liquor. The sweet aroma of anise wafted up to her from the milky liquid in the tiny glass.

It took less time to relay everything she'd seen than it did to calm down. Once the last of it passed her lips, she broke into a fresh round of sobs. Gone. Everything at the Pearl was gone.

"H-h-has Mira come here?"

"No. I haven't seen her since she told me she'd be relocating your belongings for the Saladin clan to load on the next textile wagon. They planned to smuggle you out with the silk shipment tonight."

The final shudders eased, and silence fell over her. Tears wouldn't return the dead. "Xavier Bane did this."

"Now wait a minute. Xavier isn't a murderer, and you've already said the city watch was behind it."

Rosalia clenched her jaw. "Maybe he tipped them off or paid to have us exterminated."

"I doubt it, Rosalia. I don't believe he's behind this because Xavier was here no more than a half hour ago to help *you*."

"To help me?"

"Yes. He told me about Hadrian and the others taken by the watch, but he came here specifically to save you, child. Xavier Bane is no enemy of yours and promised he wanted nothing more than to see you safe."

"I don't believe it."

"You must. Because he is a good man. One of the best I've ever known and someone I'm thankful to call friend. I simply don't believe he'd want your death over a silly trinket in his vault."

"A trinket worth thirty thousand gold coins."

"Doesn't matter. That isn't who he is. He wouldn't bring down the death of hundreds for one mirror."

A fresh wave of tears trickled over her lashes when she thought of Hadrian's corpse lying in the gutted remnants of the tavern. There had been so many memories there, her childhood gone in the blink of an eye, and so many good people slain. "How much do you trust him?"

"Enough that I made him promise to find my only daughter and bring her back to me."

Her head snapped up, vision blurred by the relentless assault.

Before she could speak, a gauntleted fist slammed against the door, metal thundering against wood. "By order of King Gregarus, open this door."

Frederico's spine straightened. He glanced away from her and rose from his seat. "Stay out of sight," he said in a low voice.

Rosalia hurried into the adjacent kitchen and squeezed into a pantry closet. It was a tight fit and stank of garlic and onions, but a narrow crack between the doors permitted her to see Frederico.

He unlatched the damaged door. The moment he did, it flew open and a half dozen royal guard stormed into the suite. They grasped him by the arms, one securing him on each side while a third held him at swordpoint.

"Where is she?" the captain demanded, standing out from the men he commanded due to the red sash across his armored chest.

"Where is who? What is the meaning of this?"

"We seek a thief. A thief who has stolen something of great significance to the crown."

"I've harbored no thieves here, only performers of various kinds. If you could be more specific? Has this thief stolen a heart, or perhaps one of my actors has run away with one of the princesses?"

The blade pressed deeper. The flesh parted beneath it and a single drop of blood welled to the surface, trickling down Frederico's neck soon after. He swallowed, throat bobbing with the motion. "Laugh now, you foolish has-been."

Frederico said nothing. He closed his eyes.

The men fanned out at the captain's order and began to search the suite, opening and closing doors, rifling through trunks. The closets opened in another room. It was a mere matter of time before they came to the pantry and discovered her.

"If you would tell me who you seek, perhaps I could share my knowledge and you'll be on your way again," Frederico said quietly.

"The thief we seek is a young woman of no great stature, dark-haired, amber eyes. We believe she goes by the name Rosalia."

Her heart jumped in her chest.

"Rosalia is my best actress, a mere performer of the art of dance. Surely you must be mistaken. I've never known her to steal."

"And yet, we have received a confession from her deceased cohorts. Several of them."

No, no, no.

"It couldn't be possible," Frederico continued.

"I believe he's told the truth, Cap'n."

"Then he's of no use to us. Execute him."

Frederico's helpless gaze darted to the pantry. He gave a subtle motion of two fingers from his restrained hand—the stage gesture for no. He meant to die for her.

Unable to watch her mentor's death, Rosalia burst from the pantry with a desperate cry on her lips. "No, I'm here! I made him conceal me."

"Ah, and our wayward prey reveals herself. A whole city turned upside down for you."

"I'll come with you peacefully. I won't fight at all. Please, just let him go."

"Peacefully, eh?" The captain nodded his head toward the two guards restraining Frederico. They released him, and the old man fell back a step to rub his wrists.

A thousand questions came to mind about why they were there for her, why the others had been slain when the royal family had known for decades about the city's criminal element—and even participated at times. According to Hadrian, the previous rulers had always given lip service to the masses about being tough on crime, but they'd never taken steps to eliminate and squash it so thoroughly before.

"Wrists out, poppet."

She obeyed. They bound her by the wrists and ankles, securing her tightly with knots she could have broken with a few minutes alone and no one breathing over her neck.

"Now we truly no longer need you, old man."

"Wait! We had a deal."

"Kill him."

One guard kicked the back of Frederick's knee, pitching the old man to the ground.

No, no, no. This wasn't how things were supposed to happen. This wasn't right.

It broke every rule.

"Please don't do this," she pleaded again. "He's innocent, he doesn't know anything more than—"

A guardsman stabbed Frederico through the chest, and a low groan of pain fell from his lips. The blade retreated then slid forward again as blooms of crimson spreading over his cream-and-gold dressing gown.

"No!" Rosalia lurched forward, startling both herself and the two men restraining her.

Then the most amazing thing occurred, and the ropes binding her wrists snapped. Howling in fury, she threw herself at the guard wielding the sword, pounding him with her fists and all of the angst she could channel into one blow. She took him off his feet, but in her tear-blinded fury, she tumbled to the floor with him and they tangled together.

The back of a gauntleted hand bounced off Rosalia's cheek, knocking her from the stunned guard and snapping her head to the side. Fresh tears welled from her eyes as her teeth crashed together and she bit her tongue. A rush of hot and salty blood filled her mouth.

Hating them and hating Xavier Bane, she fought until the same hand crashed into her face again. It knocked her senseless and took the fight out of her. The world swam in and out of focus and spun like a carousel.

"Murderers," she rasped around her swollen tongue. "Filthy bastard murderers."

The guard behind her reversed the blade in his grip and drove the hilt into the back of Rosalia's head, thrusting her into darkness.

12

BEAUTIFUL, WINGED DEATH

Rosalia startled awake to the rumbling noise of creaky wheels against hard-packed ground. She tried to move, but the manacles and chains restrained her to the wall.

Shit. It hadn't been a dream. It was really happening.

They'd said little about her fate throughout the day of imprisonment, even when they'd laughed about confiscating everything she possessed, everything she'd earned and crafted herself in the den alongside Hadrian. A guard with a lecherous, unwavering stare had watched her remove the leathers, a vulgar promise in his eyes when he'd tossed her the rough burlap shirt instead. Prison clothes. Thankfully, shift change occurred soon after, and she wasn't forced to determine whether years of picking locks and climbing walls had strengthened her hands enough to rip off a man's cock. She'd heard stories about these jails. Awful stories that didn't permit her to sleep.

Around supper time, some asshole passed her a tray with moldy bread. Worms swam in the tin water cup. She ignored it and huddled in the corner of her cell, fighting sleep deprivation.

Then a new morning came, the sun a mere golden speck on the horizon line, casting pink and lavender streaks across the dawn sky. They had dragged her to the wagon and said she'd be going straight to Sandfire Palace for execution before a private party of noble viewers and royalty.

Why had they singled her out from all the others?

And what did it matter? Escape was impossible, and the bitter taste of rock bottom discouraged her from even trying. These men were armed, and she had nothing. If she did escape, where would she go? Who would dare to take her in? She'd never make it across the blistering sands to Nairubia before succumbing to the heat.

Her closest friends, everyone she'd ever loved, and even distant associates throughout Enimura had been punished because she'd taken the wrong job. She'd never see any of them again.

It seemed so cruel a fate for one person's actions. Even if they'd all been guilty of theft at one time or another, this hadn't been their crime—Frederico, Lacherra, and Hadrian had been convicted of guilt by association.

Thinking of them tightened a vice around her throat, narrowing her breathing passage until she choked on the inevitable tears that came next. She didn't recall falling asleep during the journey from Enimura to Sandfire

Palace—mere hours by wagon—but they couldn't be far from their destination.

Why couldn't she have left the stupid glass behind and reported failure to their demanding client? Had she taken the book instead, she'd be enjoying the warmth of the ocean sun against her bare shoulders as a luxury ship carried her to some distant kingdom. Freedom could have been hers.

Tired of her sniffling, a guard banged on the wall with his fist. "Knock it off back there!"

The words "make me" died on her lips. Riling them up would only get her beaten before she reached the Royal Prison, where she was to be held until the day of her execution.

The edge of the cuffs dug into her wrists, cutting off circulation if she wriggled her hands wrong, no doubt to prevent her from picking the locks.

An alarmed cry came from the front of the wagon. "What the fuck is that?"

"It's a dragon!"

"I don't fucking believe it!"

Contrary to her original fears, she wouldn't perish on the executioner's block after all. She'd instead die some gruesome death inside of a dragon's maw. The former seemed kinder, gentler by comparison.

Someone shouted orders, a cry for the soldiers to raise their shields. A desperate plea for mercy preceded the rush of flames and the crackling of fire as it consumed its target. Then the odor of burned flesh and wood reached her nose. Instead of dying a quick death with her neck on the chopping block or in a noose, she'd roast or be crushed between a dragon's jaws.

Without warning, the top of the wagon flew off, and a scaled snout leaned over the shattered opening to peer down at her. Recognition and keen understanding shone in its green gaze, eyes larger than dinner plates in its enormous, black-scaled face. In those seconds, she realized it was the same dragon she'd encountered in the vault. The face was the same, but the scales were different. She could have sworn they were gold before.

And it was gorgeous—beautiful death on wings. This creature was an extraordinary killing machine and the last sight she'd ever see. Despite the futility of it, she cried up to the beast, "Please don't eat me!"

"Foolish, woman. Had I wanted to eat you, it would be done already," it replied in an eerily familiar voice. Was it like a parrot, adopting the accent of its owner?

"You're..." Her breath panted in and out, heart fluttering inside her chest. A dozen questions came to mind, and each of them caught in her throat. What did it want if it hadn't come to eat her? "You speak."

It pressed the tip of one talon against the thick chains connecting her manacles. Although the metal snapped under the pressure and freed her hands, the metal cuffs remained.

Rosalia stared up at him. "Why did you do that?"

The dragon plucked her from within the wagon with its left claw. The tips were as sharp as they looked, one prickling against her hip until the beast set her on the ground. Then it threw a woman's smelly corpse into the wagon where the prisoner belonged and exhaled a stream of fire until the metal links turned red hot and began to warp. "Do you want to die?"

"No!"

"Then you can stay here and await death or come with me. I won't offer again."

Looming above her, the majestic creature bowed its head and lowered to the ground. When the edge of a wing touched the soil, she realized its purpose.

Makeshift stairs. The stairway to her freedom. Behind her, she glanced at the palace in the distance and heard the wailing noise of sirens. Barefoot and unarmed, a single choice lay before her—escape or die.

Rosalia hurried up the extended wing and heaved herself onto her rescuer's back. Its initial running start jostled her despite gripping with her thighs. Years ago as a child, she'd read a fantastical book about a dragon rider and could now conclude mounting a dragon was *nothing* like riding a horse. Terrified of tumbling off to her doom, she grasped her mount by a handful of the horned growths at the base of its graceful neck and prayed the gods had mercy on her.

The ground below fell away and the distance increased, there one moment and gone in the next. Each wing flap sent the wind coursing through her dark hair, each thrust taking them a hundred feet higher.

What had taken an hour or more by wagon took mere minutes by air. The dragon landed far beyond the city outskirts, a considerable distance outside of Enimura beside an old aqueduct. Clear water splashed beneath immense claws, then it ducked down and wiggled into a dark pipeline.

"Where are we going?" Rosalia asked.

"Home. A place where no one will find you."

Wary of bumping her head against the ceiling, she flattened her body against its back and closed her eyes. *I am hugging a dragon.* And it was warm and muscular, solid beneath her with a gait smoother than glass.

The smell of clean water persisted, surrounding them with the aroma of minerals, wet metal, and damp stone. They hadn't entered the sewer at least, but one of the many freshwater sources that spilled out into the sea.

The dragon squeezed into a narrower space, leading her into deeper darkness. Eventually the cramped space expanded, and her bare legs no longer scraped the cold walls. Water dripped in the distance, and they emerged onto dry land.

Their path grew wider and something clicked in the dark.

"Hold on," he said gruffly.

He was a he, wasn't he? The beast's sonorous voice raised goose bumps over her skin, the similarity to Xavier pleasant. Familiar. His weight shifted, forcing her to tighten her hold or risk spilling from his back.

Rosalia squinted, and gradually her dark vision improved until she saw more than a mere hint of his outline. The dragon's taloned digits grasped and moved the stone, touching each block in a precise pattern. A rumbling vibrated throughout the wide corridor.

Then the wall sank, crumbling away in a fine mist of

grit and dust. He moved forward through the opening and took her into an unfamiliar network of tunnels where the air smelled clean and nothing like the rancid stink of sewer. It had taken her entire bottle of rosewater shampoo to remove the filth from her hair, and even then, Mira had insisted on combing in some jasmine tea to mask whatever odor remained.

Cool air drafted down from a chute above them, and then a tile shifted beneath the dragon's weight. Click. Click. Click. More dust, and the gate arose from the ground again to form a seamless wall behind them.

Mystified, she watched as they approached a dead end, all smooth stone with the warm yellow glow of a lantern hanging beside it, the alchemical agents within it mimicking the sun. There, he plucked her from his back and set her down, prodding her forward with the blunt curve of his claw instead of the lethal tip. "This is where your ride ends, Rosalia."

Rosalia stared at the wall. "There's nothing there." Had he brought her so far to kill her now?

The side of his wide mouth raised, revealing a hint of ivory tooth. "Isn't there?"

"It's only a wall."

"You disappoint me, little thief. I expected a brilliant mastermind capable of unraveling the greatest enchant-ments of the magical world. Yet I have a blind child before me, unable to see three feet beyond her face."

"Child?" Some of the fear faded, and anger took its place. She spun on him but was once again overwhelmed by the sheer size of the beast crowding the corridor.

Magic could be a fickle thing, and in the span of a few heartbeats her terror surged anew.

Rosalia shrank back.

The dragon scowled. "I'm not going to eat you."

"Then close your mouth and stop showing me those teeth!"

He blinked and fell back a step, lowering his head to her eye level and staring at her. "I was attempting to smile."

"You do it poorly."

I'm arguing with a dragon. Nothing about the recent turn of events in her life could be any stranger than that. Dragging in a few breaths, she forced calm into her body. Her knees quaked a few moments more, and then the uncontrollable trembling ended.

When she'd found the entrance to the vault, she'd stumbled upon it, quite literally, by accident while searching the walls for hidden levers and buttons. Instead of examining the floor, she swept the lantern from the hook and turned it upside down. The liquid contents of the alchemical device sloshed about, and the spheres floated in the glowing substance.

She prodded the bottom of it, searching for a hidden contraption, a key, anything of use.

Finding none there, she carried it to the wall and squinted while prodding for invisible crevices and lines. With a monster breathing down her neck, her control over the second sight didn't come so easily.

Then she found it. A discolored pattern on the wall at her chest height. When she raised her fingers to touch it, each digit sank through several inches of illusory wall until her hand disappeared to the wrist. Notches moved beneath her fingertips. The dragon shifted, a low chuckle rumbling in his chest.

Rosalia paused. She shifted her eyes behind her, noticing the empty space. "It's trapped isn't it."

"Astute observation."

"What happens if I dial wrong?"

"I return the pieces of you to the aqueduct."

She jerked her hand away from the wall. This time, the warmth of his laugh, heated and humid breath, washed over the back of her neck before he nudged her aside with a claw. The tips of them touched the wall, vanished through the illusion, and he made unseen gestures beneath it.

"Another time, I will teach you how to defeat this trick, but not now. I've been harsh, and this is no time to make demands of a weary woman."

The ground responded, and steps lowered into a dark, torchlit abyss. He moved ahead of her down the stairs, pressing his long body against stone to fit, though he'd seemed far too large moments ago to wiggle into the narrow space. Rosalia followed him. Once she stepped off the bottom stair, they rose toward the ceiling again and concealed that there was ever an opening at all.

"Interesting..."

"I'm glad you approve," the dragon rumbled. Genuine pleasure laced his voice without a hint of sarcasm. Undeniable pride shone in his enormous eyes.

They stood in a room within Xavier Bane's underground lair, surrounded by vast riches. Power and magic hummed through the air, raising the fine hairs on her arms, although it wasn't until she spun to face the dragon that she realized he was shrinking in size and the change in atmosphere was *him*.

As the scaled behemoth became tinier, he moved behind a screen and disappeared from sight. Seconds later, he emerged from the other side, clothed in loose trousers and pulling an oversized tunic over his head. More tattoos than she could count covered his masculine torso, each arcane glyph glowing golden in the warm candlelight amid scars that had transferred to his human flesh.

Xavier set his cool gaze on her and grinned.

All along, she'd thought Xavier commanded the dragon and kept it for a pet. Now she didn't know which idea had been more outlandish—that a dangerously handsome mage could control a dragon, or that a dragon could become a frustrating but absolutely appealing man.

13

QUESTIONS AND NEEDS

XAVIER GESTURED TOWARD THE OPEN SUITE. "MAKE yourself at home and—"

One hundred and fifteen pounds of angry, hissing, and spitting young woman threw herself at him. Her hands reached him first, taking him by surprise.

He stumbled back a step too late. She had the speed of a wild cat and the form of a person who had been taught to swing a decent right hook. He took one fist to the cheek but caught the second. Before she could lay into him again, he secured her by both wrists and yanked her body close. Part of him expected her to resort to using her teeth since he'd denied her use of her primary weapons.

Hell, that would have been hot if she had.

"Have you lost your bloody mind?"

"You were the dragon all along? You chased me through your vault!"

"You stole from my hoard."

The struggle renewed. He waited until she surrendered to his greater physical strength, slumping against him exhausted, frustrated, and even more disheveled than before. In addition to her hair hanging in a dark tangle around her face and clinging against her perspiring cheeks, she smelled of the jail.

It was not a kind scent, the odor of old bones, mold, and filthy stone on her skin.

He hated it. Hated them all for abusing her. For the bruise on her left cheek, her swollen nose, and the dried split on her lower lip. He rarely took pleasure in killing any human, but he hoped to the gods the guards he'd incinerated were the ones who'd put those injuries on her.

Deep down, he'd been terrified she would be subjected to unknown abuses while in the custody of the city watch. Several of her fellow thieves had already been executed in a variety of colorful ways. Some of their bodies still dangled from ropes in the square.

"If you're finished testing the futility of fighting with me, I'll lend you clean attire and show you to the bath."

"Why are you doing this?"

He released her. "We can discuss that later."

"To the void with that, we can discuss it now." The words trembled out of her as she fell back a step, tears shining in her eyes. "Everyone I know is dead, and I should be joining them, but... but I'm here, underground in the very place that began this entire awful mess."

"Yes."

"Why did you rescue me?"

"As I said, we can discuss this in time once you've had a chance to recuperate from your ordeal. I'm not a cruel man, so don't consider me as one. There's nothing to fear while within my domain, nothing that can harm you, no one who can find you."

"Fine."

"If you want to clean up, follow me. We can discuss any other matters after more pressing needs have been met. Unless of course, you want to remain barefoot and clothed in a burlap sack."

She nodded slowly, but the tears continued to shimmer against her long lashes. Xavier wanted to do whatever he could to banish that pain and restore a measure of the happiness he'd witnessed while she watched the singing clock in his store.

The moment Rosalia left his store, he'd pulled the clock to the work table and made the necessary adjustments, though he'd feared the worst—that he'd been an awful dinner partner—when she didn't return for it.

Had she not burglarized his shop days later, he'd planned to deliver it to the theater. The woman deserved to have it, and he'd liked the way her eyes lit with joy when the bird emerged to sing.

With her trailing behind him in silence, he led her deeper into the maze of subterranean chambers until they reached a private bedroom with its own bath in the most distant corner from the door. A few decades ago, his father had built the magical furnace and installed a network of pipes and plumbing designed to carry fresh water to the bathing rooms and kitchen. Over the years since Xavier came to Enimura, he'd improved on the outtake pipes.

She didn't utter a word, even when he crouched beside the porcelain, clawfoot tub and fiddled with the knobs until a steaming jet of water spilled from the golden faucet.

A wooden screen with pressed rice paper between the frames of the partition provided all the privacy she needed. He left her there and ventured away, returning only once to toss a fresh towel and a few garments over the top of the screen.

Aside from the gentle lapping of water against porcelain, Rosalia remained silent. She also remained in the tub until long after her skin must have wrinkled and the water had cooled.

He let her be. The woman needed time to grieve and digest the serious changes in her life.

She emerged an hour later, huddled within the modest silk nightwear and velvet dressing gown he'd lent her, the latter secured with a plum sash around her slender waist. She looked small, broken by the ordeal, and less spirited than before.

Fuck, he'd prefer her to be pounding both her fists into his chest than looking like a shattered doll. Xavier swallowed back his anxiety. "I suppose you have questions now."

Rosalia toyed with the edge of the robe and plucked the lace trimming its edge. "I do. Thank you for rescuing me, but why did you do it? Why save me when I stole from your hoard?"

"Because I need you."

———

HE NEEDED *HER*?

Trapped underground with a dragon and nowhere else to go, Rosalia stared into the face of her rescuer and wondered what price he would take from her. What favor would he ask to settle the score and erase her debt?

"Did I mishear you?" Rosalia asked after a few heart-beats of uncomfortable silence passed.

"No. I need you."

The intensity in his voice raised the fine hairs on her arms and nape. She shivered and glanced away first, breaking eye contact. "What for?"

"To take back the mirror."

"King Gregarus has it now, and gods only know where he's taken it."

"Precisely. I'm a dragon and a clockwork mechanic. I've got two main skills. Breathing fire and inventing things. Neither of those is particularly good for theft. That's your wheelhouse." The corner of his mouth raised, and his voice lowered, husky. "And you owe me. You got us into this mess. Now I want you to get us out of it and help me find it before that fool causes irreparable harm."

"It's only a piece of glass."

"No. That's where you're wrong. If it was only a piece of glass, do you think King Gregarus would have gone through so much trouble to have you acquire it? Would he have had everyone who came into contact with the bloody thing or you murdered? I imagine it's only a matter of time before some guardsman comes knocking at my door since we were seen together in public, but he wouldn't dare do to me what he did to Frederico."

Quiet, Rosalia watched him, unable to make sense of the mystery. "I... I don't know."

"There's plenty you don't know."

"If there's so much I don't know, why don't you tell me some of it instead of leaving me in the dark?"

"Follow me, and I'll explain everything."

Xavier moved away. Walking in his footstep, she entered the next room and followed him down a narrow walkway. She'd encountered him for the first time in the same chamber, unaware of a dragon's presence due to the sheer amount of wealth overflowing from the pits on each side. He must have been slumbering beneath it all.

Instead of heading straight ahead to the altar in the distance, he turned left and directed her into another room that resembled a gentleman's study complete with a writing desk pushed against the wall flanked by two bookshelves.

The cozy chamber had all the comforts of a bedroom but no bed. Instead, piles of cushions occupied a corner of the floor and a magical pit filled with enchanted stones imitated a charcoal hearth. Silk rugs and ornate tapestries hung on the stone walls, and gilded sconces glowed with magical fire.

Unable to help herself, Rosalia drifted closer to touch a fixture fastened to the wall. Each room had its own theme and design, touched by the style of another kingdom. These were elvish. "This is beautiful," she murmured.

"Thank you?"

Her eyes turned to him and took in his startled expression. Feeling churlish and unappreciative of his generosity, she cleared her throat and drifted to her host. He'd saved her from certain death and dismemberment, all because she'd taken the wrong job.

But if she hadn't accepted the contract, one of the other Pearls would have taken it. Hadrian might have even undertaken the task himself, and she had doubts that he could have outrun a dragon. She shivered.

Would Xavier have eaten him?

"Are you warm?"

"Very. Thank you."

"You're shivering."

"I'm reminded of how close I came to death or slavery."

"They're one and the same."

Rosalia tucked her chin. "Yes."

Xavier gestured to the short sofa beside his desk. She settled on it with her hands on her lap and examined her surroundings.

There were glass orbs floating above stone pedestals, crackling bolts of lightning arcing within them. Nearby, a row of candles each sported a different color flame. The room was rich with art and color, with beauty and elegance, teeming with magical design she didn't comprehend though those flames called to her.

"Thank you."

Xavier took the seat at his desk and angled the chair toward her. "You're welcome."

"You didn't have to save me."

"But I did, and as I said, I need you."

"Regardless. Your generosity is beyond necessity, and I haven't been gracious. I realize that now."

"But it isn't," he disagreed. "You're in need, and I have something to give. Contrary to whatever myth has painted of dragons, we're not all greedy." Appearing to realize the irony in his statement, he glanced toward the open doorway. Gold shone through the arch and shimmered beneath the torches.

"How did you move so much gold beneath this shop?"

"A combination of magic and actual labor. Much of it was... shipped to me from a prior hoard, but the rest has come over the past three years of operating in this city. I spend little, I travel infrequently, and I enjoy no company but my own."

Until he met her. Guilt tugged Rosalia's heart until she studied the cool stone beneath her feet. He'd given her slippers, but the soft velvet only cushioned her steps without providing any warmth. As she wrung her hands, she glanced up to find him watching her in return, the pen still against the stationary paper. "I—"

"Food may make the conversation we're to have more palatable. Are you hungry?"

"*Yes.*"

With the fear of imminent death behind her, Rosalia's appetite had finally returned.

Xavier rose from his seat. "I'll return shortly."

"Where are you going?"

"You wouldn't enjoy the food available in the hoard. The rest is in the cold box and larder upstairs. Feel free to have a look around."

Rosalia tilted her head. "Aren't you worried I'll steal something."

"And put it where?" His eyes dropped to the silk pajamas and dressing gown covering her. It clung to her curves in all the right places, concealing and revealing everything at once. "And if you do steal it, where are you going to go? The sewer again? And if you do reach it and escape into the city, what then? No one will take you in, and you'll only perish in the desert."

When his gaze raked over her, Xavier didn't have a mere look. He devoured her with his eyes. Part of her wondered why a dragon owned such beautiful and feminine garments, but she feared the truth wouldn't be as delicious as the mystery.

She wondered if there been a woman in his life at some point, preferring to think he'd had a lover at one point over believing he had a fondness for collecting women's undergarments.

Rosalia pondered that after he left. While he was gone, she racked her brain over his behavior during their meeting in the shop. He'd been friendly and kind to her, interested in her dancing, and even flirtatious, but she hadn't picked up anything that implied he'd take her to bed until his blundering invitation to dinner.

And what an evening it had been, gazing into those

beautiful eyes and becoming lost in a field of endless turquoise. Despite Adriano's interest in her, she'd never felt truly desired until she was across a table from Xavier, wondering what the hell she'd done to earn the attention of a skilled sorcerer.

Xavier returned with a platter of diced cheese, sliced sausage, and a thick chunk of fluffy, moist bread that compressed like a sponge when she pressed it with a finger.

Then he set a bottle of wine down on the desk, popped the cork with his thumb—she'd never seen anyone do that before—and poured her a glass after a fine mist of fragrant air escaped from it.

Rosalia stuffed her face and ate until her belly approached the point of near bursting. Indecision divided her between setting the empty platter aside and licking the smear of honey that remained on it.

He glanced at her. "Would you like more?"

"No, thank you. I shouldn't."

He took the platter from her. A deft movement of his fingers vanished it in a puff of black smoke and a few golden sparks. "I understand that you have many questions, and I will answer each of them to the best of my knowledge. This lair is a safe place, protected by magic no common sorcerer could ever unravel."

"I did it without being a sorcerer."

"You're different."

"Why did you save me? Why do you *need* me?"

"I knew your mother."

The floor dropped out from beneath her, and she

wasn't sure if she wanted to believe him or call him a liar to his face. Aside from Hadrian, Lacherra, Adriano's mother, and a handful of thieves in their company, she'd never spoke to anyone who knew her mother before. She swallowed, willing her throat to cooperate. "*When* did you meet her? My mother has been dead for twenty years. I was a child when she passed away."

He nodded. "The death of your mother was an unfortunate and terrible loss. Trust me when I say she was mourned by many beyond the den of thieves you called home. News of her passing traveled as far as Ilyria, and she left behind a hole no one has been able to fill until now."

Rosalia clutched both hands against her lap. "Until now?"

"You. I returned to Enimura five years ago seeking you."

A bitter laugh shook her shoulders. "You've had plenty of time to find me. I perform on stage three nights a week."

"You perform under a stage name, and you keep to the shadows. When I saw you on stage a few nights past, I found myself intrigued, but it wasn't until you broke into my hoard—until you penetrated more than a dozen layers of magical security—that I *knew* you must be Dahlia's child. Not only do you resemble her, but you have her gifts."

"Let's pretend that I believe you've sought me. Why? What's so special about me that you needed to find me?"

"Your mother smuggled the mirror into my possession

many years ago." He leaned forward. "It was given to her by our now deceased king, father of the dictator now sitting the throne. He knew his son would become a tyrant when he came into power, but the traditions of the royal family are set in stone by unbreakable laws."

The longer she listened to his story, the queasier she became. Could it be true? Xavier gazed at her with sad eyes, earnest expression reaching through the defensive shield built by years of skepticism. "What's so important about this thing? Why was he willing to pay thirty thousand ducats for a piece of glass?"

"It's more than a piece of glass. What you took is an ancient relic once guarded in the Royal Family Vault." Xavier eased back in his chair. "It is said, years ago when the gods fought and warred with the forces of the demonic plane, Iblis himself also walked this desert. When he was vanquished by Arcadian the Bright, the ground beneath him smoldered as he passed from our physical realm and returned to Gehenna where he belongs. But at that site, the sand itself became a thin pane of glass. Stories say a single shard survived and was fashioned by an artisan into a mirror."

Rosalia's eyes widened. "The Devil's Eyeglass."

"Yes. A cursed mirror able to open the door between Gehenna and Ordania—our world."

14

MORE THAN LUCK

THIS TIME ROSALIA LAUGHED, TOSSING BACK HER head at the absurd notion. "There's no way you could possibly believe the Devil's Eyeglass exists. It's a *myth* about greed, vanity, and evil. Girls are always told if they gaze too long in the mirror, Iblis will take them for his bride. That's why there are no mirrors in the temples devoted to Arcadian."

Xavier chuckled. "I'm familiar with the fables, but I assure you, the mirror *does* exist and is now in the hands of our common enemy."

"How do you know? Were you there to see it? Are you a two-thousand-year-old mummy dragon?"

The amusement in his eyes faded. He leaned forward, gaze hard. "Sixty-three, and no, I was not there. My grandfather was present, because he's the bastard who framed the mirror."

She quieted for a moment. "When you say that my

mother smuggled it to you, when did this happen? How do I know you're not mistaken?"

"Your mother's name was Dahlia, and what transpired was only months prior to your birth."

She quieted. He knew her mother's name.

"I was only a young dragon then, and newly on my own. She sought my father at the advice of the elf queen, but he had perished during the war between Ilyria and Nairubia years prior to that, leaving only me in his hoard. I became the keeper of the mirror, and she returned to this cesspool at some point with you. Before that, your father, whoever he was, had already died in the service of the king."

"Now I know you're lying. I knew my father. I *remember* him. My father was a pompous asshole who mistreated us. She left him."

His lips twitched. "I have no reason to lie about what I recall of my brief acquaintance with your mother, Rosa. When I met her, she was already with child *and* in mourning. Whoever you know as your father was some other man."

Her entire world crumbled, reduced to broken promises and lies. For a moment, she hated him. Wanted to scratch out his eyes and claw him and kick and scream and hit. Everything she'd ever known about her life evaporated and left a hollow, aching place in her chest.

"I don't understand..."

He didn't rush her. Crushing silence fell between them until Xavier leaned close enough to take her by one hand. He tenderly stroked her knuckles. "I'm sorry to be the bearer of bad news, but it is what it is. She risked both of your lives to deliver the mirror to Ilyria. I haven't lied to you yet, and I don't intend to start now."

It wasn't his fault if she'd been raised believing in a lie. She swallowed back a sob and nodded before swiping her other hand across her cheeks. "I understand. About the mirror, why would King Gregarus trust it to the elves? Enimura hates elves. They barely tolerate even the wealthy ones, and even then, only for the money they bring to the city."

Xavier sighed and leaned back in his seat, releasing her fingers. "Two things, sweetling. He didn't trust it to the elves, and technically, I'm not one of them. I'm a weredragon, to be specific."

Rosalia blinked up at him, the term something she'd only ever heard in fairy tales. "Weredragons are *real*?"

"Yes, we are. King Gregarus trusted the mirror to my kind, hoping we would guard it. Somehow, news of its whereabouts must have returned to the current king."

"It did. Grandmaster Ombre passed the contract to our gang for completion, because he knew we had some of the best burglars in the guild."

He stroked his chin. "What I want to know is why there isn't a platoon of soldiers beating on my door if they knew where to find it all this time."

"No. They didn't know *who* had it. We were merely told it had been smuggled into the hands of a clockwork mechanic years ago. We visited dozens of shops before locating it. In fact... I lied to my friend initially. After I determined you had to be the one holding it, I fibbed and said your place had nothing of value. I led her to believe I found the mirror elsewhere, because she would have sold the information of your riches to every burglar across Enimura."

"You told no one else?"

"Only Hadrian, and he's dead now. He'd have taken it to his grave. He's good like that. Lacherra always tried to get him to speak up about jobs, and he'd only laugh and kiss her, say if she wanted to know thief's business, she should have remained a thief."

His brows shot up. "I see. I suppose I should thank you, although you've benefitted as much from your discretion as I have."

A few tears slid down her cheeks. She hastily scrubbed them away with her palm and gave him a hard look. "You said you've been seeking me before this happened? Why? What's so special about me?"

"You don't know?"

"Know what?"

Xavier leaned forward. "Your mother wasn't a mere human or thief. She was a djinn, a spirit of air and fire capable of bending the laws of fortune to her whim. More than that, she was the personal assassin of Queen Morwen."

The laughter bubbled out of her at once. "That's ridiculous. I would know if my mother wasn't human—if *I* wasn't human."

"You're not," he persisted.

"Trust me. I'd know if I was... some elemental creature. I feel human."

"Half, and you wouldn't know. Your gifts are of a subtle nature, subconsciously affecting the currents of fate and fortune unlike a magician actively casting spells. This is why so many things work in your favor. Tell me, Rosalia, how many times in your career have you just barely scraped by out of a shit situation?"

"Many, but that's just luck."

"Djinn's luck. You can taste magic, can't you? Feel it in the air and know things other thieves never know."

"I call it intuition."

Xavier stared at her, dark brows drawing closer together. "Bullshit. You blundered your way into my lair through countless magical traps. If you can believe I'm a weredragon, and if you can believe the truth about the mirror, why not believe this about yourself?"

Her hands trembled. She fisted both against her thighs to disguise it and sat ramrod straight, lifting her chin and meeting his stare head-on without blinking or averting her gaze. "Perhaps I don't even believe you about the mirror. Why would King Gregarus go through so much effort and abolish his city's Thieves Guild for one mirror?"

"The man who wields the Devil's Eyeglass commands the armies of Gehenna. He's a dictator, and he thirsts for a war he can't lose. Enimura has been at odds with Ilyria for years since his father died."

"But never at war."

The corner of his mouth rose. "Because the elven armies outnumber Enimura's military five to one, and when it comes to skill, King Gregarus's cavalry can't outperform mounted archers from my homeland. But demons... that's an entirely different matter."

She failed to suppress a shudder. "I don't want to believe it's true."

"Refusing to believe it won't make it any less so. And now you know the value of the item you took and the importance of reclaiming it."

Rosalia moistened her lips and considered the unspoken *and* spoken words between them. He wanted to retake the mirror from the royal family. By now, it would be in the king's possession, no doubt returned to the vault where it belonged. "It was safe in the Royal Vault before for hundreds of years. We don't know that the current king will misuse it."

"I have one more thing to tell you."

"What? What else could there possibly be?"

"The royal guard, while thorough and bloodthirsty, chose not to murder every thief they encountered. Some were taken captive and jailed for their crimes against the crown, but they weren't executed at the square either."

If she'd been standing, her legs might have given out beneath her. His words slammed the breath from her lungs and brought fresh, hot tears coursing down her cheeks. "Someone survived the purge?"

"Several. I couldn't tell you their names, but the current gossip at the markets is favorable for your kin."

"I don't understand. Why was I separated from the others if we were all found guilty of theft?"

Xavier took her hand and cupped it between his

palms, long fingers stroking her knuckles. "You were separated from the others due to the extreme nature of your supposed crimes. Because they charged you for more than theft, Rosalia. They accuse you of treason, saying you've colluded with the elven government. They claim you gutted Frederico after murdering your flatmate."

A sick feeling punched her in the gut, raising bile in her throat. She couldn't blink back the tears this time. "I watched them kill Frederico. They cut him down for providing shelter to me. As for Mira, I'd... I'd never hurt her. We may have disagreed at times, but I loved her. She was my *sister*. My friend."

"I believe you. According to them, you're a spy for Ilyria, and slew Frederico when he warned the royal guard about your treachery."

"And Mira?"

Xavier sighed. "I... found her body. Someone murdered her then began a fire to cover it up. Your landlady and all who lived there lost their homes."

He poured her another glass of wine and pushed it between her hands. She sipped it gratefully and let the sweet vintage carry the sour taste of grief away.

Xavier didn't rush her to speak. He set a fresh parchment sheet on the desk and began writing in an unfamiliar, looping script.

"Why would they do this? Why blame me for his death? Why blame me for Mira?"

"I don't know and can only speculate. It's possible the king's spymaster saw you as a threat to be removed from the equation and a scapegoat as well. I recognized you for what you are when I saw you dance on stage."

"That's ridiculous. I look like any other woman."

"Far from it. But your beauty has nothing to do with my recognition of you as a half-djinn." And then his smoldering gaze studied her with all the intensity she'd enjoyed during their evening out. It sent heat curling in the pit of her stomach and warmth flushing over her face. She glanced away first, conflicted by the tumultuous emotions that demanded for her to mourn yet feel flattered by his compliments.

"So if you and this spymaster were able to see it, why hasn't Mira's boyfriend noticed? She dated a mage."

"Skill levels vary among practitioners of magic. How could he determine your magical ancestry if he'd never met a djinn before in the past? Could you differentiate wine from rum with a sip if you had never tasted either?" His fair brows rose.

"I suppose not."

"Such is the case of magical beings and creatures such as us."

"I see nothing unusual about you when I look at you. Sometimes there's a subtle glow, or..." She gazed at him, lost in his eyes again. There was always a hint of a molten heat, like candle flame dancing behind a pane of emerald stained glass.

"Or?" he prompted.

"I see it in your eyes. Not always, but sometimes when you look at me, I can see it."

A satisfied smile came over his face. "Astute observation."

If some of her fellow thieves were alive, that meant they were awaiting a rescue. Hope and despair intermingled and became one warring force complicated by fear of landing behind bars and resuming her figurative stroll to the chopping block.

"I lost all of my gear, Xavier. Without my weapons and my armor, I'm nothing."

"Bullshit," he growled. The word rumbled in his chest and raised the hairs on the back of her neck, breaking her arms out in goose bumps. "The cloak isn't your knowledge. Those daggers aren't your skill. They're merely a costume. Tools."

"And without my tools, I'll never travel this city unnoticed, no matter how lucky you believe me to be. Although I was never tried or judged, they declared me to be a murderess. Anyone could recognize my face."

Xavier leaned forward. "Have you ever considered that the items you carried are not as unique as you believed them to be?"

"Many of my items were made for me. Special."

Rising, he gestured for her to follow. His long-legged stride ate up the floor, forcing her to jog and catch up.

"How long did it take to build this?"

"I couldn't tell you."

"Did you not keep track?"

"No, I couldn't tell you, because I didn't build this hoard. There are many places like this across the world, each one carved by a dragon years ago. Sometimes they're centuries old. My kind may be solitary creatures, but we're not as greedy as the legends would paint us to be."

"You share homes?"

"Yes. We travel the world and visit distant places, and when we find a land we enjoy, we build a home there. Perhaps a century later, we will gift it to our young or abandon it for the next dragon to find, taking with us only the things we loved most."

"How do you find these places?"

He stopped and placed a hand on an empty section of flawless stone wall. A wave of cobalt spread beneath the pressure and flashed with magic, resembling a living, breathing force. The ebb and flow continued until the section of wall melted away like the receding tide and left only an empty arch. "We leave messages for one another in scent and dragonscript—messages no one but our kind can see from the air or below on the ground."

And then he stepped aside and ushered her into an armory glittering with unknown delights.

———

XAVIER WATCHED Rosalia's eyes grow wide with wonder. She took slow steps forward into the chamber and traced her fingers over conditioned leather and metal polished to a smooth, mirrored shine. There was very little dust within this hoard because most items within were enchanted to some degree. The very essence of magic repelled rust and grime.

"This is... I've never seen an armory of this type before."

He grinned. "You've never visited a dragon's hoard."

Stuffed dummies throughout the room sported the best pieces of equipment, some of them taken off the corpses of adventurers too dimwitted to stand down when facing a dragon.

"Dragons are packrats. When we see shiny objects, we must have them. Likewise, when foolish humans challenge a dragon in his home, we keep what we desire of their belongings. What you see here are weapons passed down through several generations of my family. Whenever I move, I take my favorite pieces with me."

She spun to stare at him. "How many times have you moved your home?"

"Only twice before. I have another lair across the sea in Utopia that I carved with my own claws. This once belonged to my grandfather, and the hoard in Ilyria is my father's home. But now, this land suits my purposes. I needed to find you since I suspected you would have grown up by now, so I waited until the fated day when we would cross paths."

Drawn by the shine of a dagger on a shelf, she drifted away from him toward a row of weapon stands holding blades charged with a variety of spell effects. She lifted one dagger and traced her thumb over the flat of the blade. "Your patience is enviable."

"Thanks. I think. Anyway, take what you need. And if your luck persists, the Master of Fate will lead you to your confiscated belongings. I have no doubt they would fetch a few ducats on the market."

Rosalia touched a shimmering cloak hanging from a dress mannequin. The material had been woven from the black silk of the shadowgliders that inhabited the Gloomshade Forest bordering elven lands. There, the enormous moth larvae spun cocoons larger than grown men, and the elves gathered the silk to make fine clothing desired across the eleven kingdoms.

"They'll have sold it all by now. Magical goods and items go for a fair price in Enimura."

"Maybe. Maybe not. We won't know until we go to rescue your friends."

She jerked around to stare at him, lowering her hand from the cloak. "We?"

"Did you think I intended to let you go alone?"

"You're not a thief. What good are you to me if you draw suspicion upon yourself?"

Xavier chuckled. "Give me a little credit, would you?"

Rosalia folded her arms against her chest and gave him a long stare. "You're dressed like a wealthy merchant, you're twice my height—"

"Exaggeration." He had maybe six inches on her, but still, he was rather tall for an elf.

"—elven, and easy to spot in a crowd."

"I didn't intend to traipse behind you like a bloody shadow."

"And your fair skin draws attention to you in a kingdom of people who are brown, just to let you know."

Xavier pressed his mouth into a thin line. Amusement flickered in her eyes, a hint of mirth he'd wanted to see returned to her expression, but not at his expense. "I'm well aware of that, and while I'm unable to change the appearance of my current state, I *can* do this."

The rainbow dragons of Ilyria had the ability to change appearance on a whim when in their draconic forms. It was a well-kept secret among them, shared among few people outside of their kind. But for Rosalia, he was willing to give everything.

The change swept over his body from head to toe once he chose the form he wanted to adopt. Concentration shunted the enormous bulk of his mass and dispersed it into the cosmos, stowed away until it became necessary to assume his man shape again.

From the ground, he gazed up at her, no larger than a desert sand monitor but certainly deadlier.

15

THE FIERCEST RAINBOW

HER MOUTH FELL OPEN. THE MIGHTY DRAGON SHE'D expected to accompany her was as large as her hand and no longer the shade of volcanic glass. Now he was burnished gold, like sunlight and rainbows given physical form.

Rosalia crouched and offered him a hand, thrilled when he crawled from the pile of clothing onto her palm. He couldn't have weighed more than a pound or two.

"You're small." Unable to resist, she traced one finger down his back between his wings, which were soft to the touch like worn suede broken in over the course of many winters.

"I am a rainbow dragon. My particular breed has many gifts, ability to manipulate our size and color the least of our talents."

She wanted to rub her cheeks against his body, wanted to feel the warmth of him against her skin and inhale the rich aroma of smoke and sand that seemed to be part of his very being. "You're... adorable."

Draconic faces were quite expressive when one had the time and inclination to admire them, easier when they weren't showing two dozen foot-long teeth. His snout wrinkled back and revealed a few of them. They'd been reduced to a size smaller than toothpicks. "Dragons are not adorable," he disagreed, bristling. A few of his scales raised along his back, until he resembled a surly cat.

"When they're palm-sized, they are."

Xavier snorted, releasing twin plumes of dark smoke from his narrow nostrils.

"You'll stand out though unless I tuck you somewhere."

He sighed. His entire body wiggled from side to side and a transformation swept down his form from nose to tail. Before her eyes, the copper-gold shade darkened until he was blacker than coal and a miniature of the form that had chased and rescued her. Only his eyes shone vermillion. "Is this better?"

"I... Yes. It is. I believe this will work."

"Excellent. I'll retake my other form again."

Xavier glided down from her open hand to the floor. Realizing the pile of clothing wouldn't reappear on his body, she spun and placed her back to him.

"Shy?"

"Not at all. It's just awkward having an important discussion with a man you barely know when he's dangling around in your face."

He chuckled. Silence fell between them as clothing rustled. Finally, he spoke up. "I'm decent."

She twisted around to face a man again, a fine and handsome man with ears that tapered at the tips with delicate points, visible beneath the wild spill of his blue-black hair. Depending on how the light hit it, there were strands of amber and violet amidst his hair. It took all her control not to step forward and run her fingers through it to find the rainbow again.

"Now, as I was saying before that demonstration, there are many things here that'll suit your needs." He removed the cloak she'd admired and placed it around her shoulders. It shimmered and took on the appearance of their surroundings. The back of his hand grazed her cheek. A knuckle skimmed her jaw. She bit her tongue and watched him.

"It fits as if it had been made for you," he said in a soft voice. "Is it not better than the cloak you wore when you visited my vault?"

A breath shuddered from her. A shadowglider cloak would have cost her hundreds of gold coins, and even then, the matter of supply and demand made them impossible to find. The elves guarded their silk farms jealously and harvested limited amounts each season. "It is."

"What's wrong?"

"It's a beautiful gift. Almost too great to accept."

"Then consider it a loan and repay me."

"With what? I have nothing."

"By reacquiring the mirror and rescuing your friends."

Rosalia blinked a few times and nodded. "I will. For what it's worth, I'm sorry that I took the job. If I'd known... if I had realized what it was—"

He touched her chin and raised her face until their gazes met. "You would have taken it anyway. No one believes the old stories anymore. They're myth. Legends. Fables told by the old and superstitious to a generation who refuses to believe. Now, are you ready to view the rest of the armory or shall we stand here admiring your fine new cloak until nightfall?"

A bit of laughter bubbled from her. Gods, it felt good to laugh after so much misery and pain. She followed him deeper into the armory. Many of the weapons appeared to be nothing unusual, the collection of old longswords peppered with unfamiliar armaments she'd never seen before.

"You'll need boots and practical gear. While we can darken anything with soot if it's inappropriate in color, the fit is what concerns me. Ah, here. These are dwarven leather, sized to their people."

He offered her a pair of glossy leather boots. She tried one on and wiggled her toes, forced to tighten the laces for them to hug her shins. "Not too thick in the sole, but definitely inflexible."

Xavier drew a shining dagger from a wooden case with a glass lid. "Leave that to me. I'll break them in. This is an elvish *anellan*, also known as a snake's fang. See this groove?" He touched a groove along the edge of the curved blade. "It's designed to hold poison."

"Why do you collect so many things?"

"Why do thieves steal?"

"Because we're assholes?"

He opened and shut his mouth, a moment of silence passing before a deep belly chuckle shook his shoulders. "No, I meant to say because it is in our nature. As I said before, we are packrats, and it's part of who we are. When I see a beautiful thing, I feel compelled to have it. To protect it."

The way he gazed at her turned her legs boneless. He may as well have transmorphed them with a flesh-to-water spell or some other rubbish.

Dammit. Stop staring at him. "Most of this is junk," she blurted inelegantly.

His eyes twinkled with humor. "It is, but as I said before, it's been acquired over generations of knights and armored adventurers hoping to find plunder in a dragon's lair. Sometimes I melt down the metal again for use in my work."

Rosalia shuddered. "That's disgusting."

"Be thankful I've removed some of the skeletons that once inhabited them."

She stared at him.

Hours later, after Xavier had taken in the seams on a leather tunic and blackened the rest of her new gear with soot, Rosalia stood at the entrance of the aqueduct, wondering how the hell she could accomplish the impossible.

Most people couldn't wait to escape jail. She had to break in to one.

16

A VALUABLE WEAPON

THE JAIL WAS A DARK, DANK PLACE BENEATH THE barracks where the city watchmen lived, reported for duty, and took complaints from citizens. It would be crawling with guards wielding truncheons and swords, every one of them familiar with Rosalia's face and ready to pummel her into a fine paste if she was found on the premises.

Until two days ago, she'd never seen the inside of it before. Thieves went out of their way to avoid it. It wasn't that they were too smart to steal from the watch—many of her blackguard brothers were cunning enough to ease the purse off a watchman's belt if they were so inclined. On his worst day prior to his injury, Hadrian had the finesse and sleight of hand to steal a watchman's smallclothes and leave a banana wedged between his cheeks.

The problem with the watch barracks had nothing to do with a lack of cunning, talent, or courage from her light-fingered mates, and everything to do with the mysteries beyond its steel doors and the two dozen men inside who knew its every inch, blind spot, and corner. Thieves couldn't work in certainties, but they also liked to learn as much about a job as they could through observation, study, and casing a mark before springing their plans. Shy of stealing a uniform and praying the others didn't recognize the stranger in their midst, she'd never heard anyone devise a clever stratagem to safely enter the building.

And a thief without a plan didn't remain in the career for long.

Rosalia sighed, gazing up at three stories of sandstone brick. Each entrance—and presumably the corridors as well—was lit with alchemical lanterns enchanted to make thieves soot glow brighter than emberfly larvae. "This feels like a poor idea."

Did she really need friends?

"If rescuing your friends from the executioner's block isn't great enough motivation, perhaps I should appeal to your greed. Do you want your things or not?" Xavier's voice sounded tiny in her ear. The way he'd curled around her neck and held on prickled his claws against her skin, a mere annoyance but solid reminder that there was a tiny dragon clinging inside her hood.

A tiny fucking dragon. Of all the adventures she'd ever undertaken across the city, she'd never have bet for a thousand ducats that she'd be infiltrating a prison in the company of a weredragon.

Despite her advantages, the place may as well have been a fortress or Sandfire Palace itself. Only a single thief had breached those walls before, and he'd claimed the halls within were a twisting maze patrolled by a man in every corridor. When another man attempted to recreate his fortunate journey to the beyond and back, he was found and made an example of by the night's watch on the next morning, drawn and quartered before an eager crowd after the magistrate had his say.

The people of Enimura loved an execution, and a thief's execution was favored above all.

"Of course I want my things, you bloody scaled git. I'd just prefer if I didn't walk into the execution you saved me from. And... I do want my friends."

"You won't be caught. And if you were, I'll get us out of it as I explained before."

As much as she'd love for Xavier to crash into the building and rip the roof off the barracks, it would only raise the citywide alarm, and there'd be dozens of soldiers there within minutes to fend him off with bows and enchanted steel. Dragons, while tough, weren't impenetrable.

Which was why he'd devised a plan to infiltrate the building, incapacitate the guards with a sleeping charm, and then use a little earth magic to burst into the sewer system under the jail. They'd be in and out before the city watchmen knew their captives had flown the coop.

With a devious, problem-solving mind like that, Rosalia thought he would have made an excellent thief.

Rosalia's palms began sweating inside her kidskin gloves. She missed her old ones made from absorbent shadowscale hide or even the fancy pair she'd borrowed from Mira. Those were the very same gloves she'd been wearing at the time of her capture. "Are you certain I won't glow beneath the alchemical lamps?"

"I swear upon all the gold in my hoard. Wait here for a moment while I scout ahead. There's an open window on the third floor."

Xavier hurried away and scaled the wall with ease, his small toes silent against the sandstone bricks. By the time he returned, she'd started to fret over his absence, waiting any moment for shouts from within the barracks. She crouched and scooped him up again, placing the palm-sized dragon on her shoulder.

"Well?"

"I was right. Most of the watchmen are asleep. According to the roster, they've already had the evening shift change." A wide grin spread across his reptilian face, revealing many of his teeth. "I had a peek."

"What's behind that window?"

"Sleeping quarters. While I was scouting ahead, I overheard that most confiscated goods go to the jailor's office before redistribution and auction, but burglary is not my forte."

"But it is mine."

He shot her a look, reptilian eyes narrowing. "As I am well aware." She swallowed down the sour taste of shame in her throat. He was within his right to hold that against her. "There was also no way I could sneak it out without someone noticing a fairy dragon with a bundle of stolen goods. There's one thing, however."

"What?"

He hesitated a moment. "Your friends. They're not here. Cells are all empty."

"What?"

"They were here until this evening, but they're gone now. All I know is they weren't executed. I could have hung around for a while longer to eavesdrop, but I wasn't comfortable with leaving you here alone to wait."

"Then I'll have to go in and find out."

Rosalia stared at the open window above them. They were framed by a set of heavy curtains with reflective white sides designed to keep rooms cool and dark during the scorching sunlight hours, ideal for men who worked nights and slept during days. Sleeping quarters meant tired guards, and tired guards weren't likely to notice her. Finding handholds in the bricks, she climbed up the wall and eased through the open window.

Two rows of identical cots stretched across the barracks floor, but only a quarter were empty. Men in varying states of dress occupied the others, most clad in only their smallclothes or short breeches. The room smelled of maleness, tobacco, and Nairubian musk oil, a favorable scent of the season used by many bachelors of low-to-middle class wealth.

Crouching, she made her way across the room's perimeter while praying to the twin god and goddess for luck. Though if Xavier could be trusted, she made her own luck and needed no additional blessings from Inja and Islena.

Most of the candle lights had been extinguished save for a couple on bedside tables on the distant side of the

room. Another stroke of luck had placed the window and
the open door in a favorable position, granting her a
direct route from the dormitory room. Unnoticed by all,
she snuck into a corridor with five other doors, only two
of them shut. A man stood with his back to her in one,
chatting with another watchman.

"What'll we do now that there are no thieves to take
bribes from? I don't know if I can support my family on
this pay alone."

Rosalia wrinkled her nose. It was nice to see where
the concerns of the watch lay after carrying out genocide
against an entire subset of the city's people. All of her
friends were dead or imprisoned, and he was worrying
about his purse.

His companion chuckled. "Nobody told you to go
and have eight children. Wages aren't all that bad."

"Speak for yourself. You've got lieutenant's pay at
least. The salary of a mere watch sergeant is barely a few
silvers more than common pay."

After ducking down low, she swept past the talkative
pair and toward the end of the hall where the staircase
descended to a landing lit by a single lantern. Trusting
Xavier's magic, she hugged the wall and made her
way down.

"You'll take the staircase to the lower floor," Xavier
whispered. "There, you'll find a door leading to the
prison level where the head jailor keeps his office. He's
away at the moment, facilitating some kind of exchange. I
didn't remain long enough to overhear everything.

"Blast."

Too bad she couldn't see through his eyes like a proper familiar. She'd heard of mages who had such pets, using their animal's sense of smell, hearing, and sight by imbuing a portion of their own soul into the creature. Then again, she didn't want her soul tangled with Xavier's at all in any way.

Nearing the landing with the enchanted lantern had an unexpected, opposite effect on her cloak. The shadows gathered around her, and the light dimmed. She lingered for a second, fascinated by the way it muffed the alchemical device.

"I told you."

Smug bastard. She ignored his little voice, even if she wanted to grab him from within her hood and kiss his scaled face over and over. When she resumed her path to the ground floor, the building's acoustics carried voices to her from below. The low murmur grew in volume, then three men appeared, bringing with them the scent of smoke and sweat. Panic beat behind her breast with the force of a dozen galloping horses. There was nowhere to go, nowhere to hide.

"Down, quickly," Xavier hissed in her ear. "Become as small as you can."

Rosalia dropped into a low crouch and tucked her body into the fetal position with the cloak thrown over her. It was cool beneath it. Somehow, the double layers of fabric didn't dim her sight beyond its black silk.

"Can't believe a dragon is in Saudonia. How long do you think it will take before the hunters locate and slay it?"

"Days perhaps. Once the hunters arrive and get on the trail, its days will be numbered. I heard the king hired the best."

"Yeah?"

The conversation came upon her, growing louder as both men passed her on the stairwell, blind to her presence. Their voices trailed and grew softer when they reached the top of the stairs. Seconds later, they were gone, leaving only her and Xavier behind.

"They're looking for you."

"Yeah, best of luck to them. I'm not a common dragon, and I'm not foolish enough to be found where they'll search for me."

"Later, you'll have to explain the damned difference between your different breeds."

The staircase let out into a short corridor beside the office of the city watch—a big room with three desks often manned by bored men who sometimes alternated between taking bribes and occasionally promising some poor citizen they'd send an officer to investigate the alleged crime.

Of course, all watchmen weren't bad or corrupt. There were just as many who weren't on the take, good men and women who actually did their jobs and forced the leaders of the complicated guild system to work. In those cases, when an unfortunate thief went before the magistrate, they received a swat on the wrist for their misbehavior.

"There." The warmth of his whisper skimmed her cheek. "Enter the door behind the watch sergeant's desk."

She snuck past the lone watchman and infiltrated the dungeon with ease, thanking her lucky stars the sergeant had been upstairs running his mouth. The smell of mildew and wet stone filled the air from a recent rain. They'd had plenty of it, and a steady drip echoed from some distant location.

Keeping to the shadows, Rosalia avoided a patrolling jailer and took Xavier's directions to the warden's office. Two levels of cells and twisting passages created Enimura's jail, though most were empty because the people, as well as their kingdom's new monarch, preferred a good hanging over letting anyone serve out their time.

So much had changed under the rule of the new king. His father would have never allowed such a perversion of justice to occur. They may have been thieves, but they served a purpose in the greater scheme of life, and their activity had always been monitored.

The warden's office was near the entrance of the jail, only one passage over from the stairway. She breathed a sigh of relief and ducked inside the unlocked room, so thankful she could have cried.

A single window was behind the messy desk, a rectangular, two-foot-long opening near the ceiling revealing the lantern-lit city streets outside and the fat, silver moon in the bleak sky. Beneath the window and tucked beside a bookshelf, she saw a sturdy wooden chest.

Rosalia removed the pickset she'd foraged from Xavier's equipment room and frowned at the pieces. They were superior to her old tools in every way, feeling light and comfortable in her hand. She wiggled them into the lock and finagled the pins with ease. Lifting the lid away revealed a bundle of leathers and several purses she hadn't taken. Rosalia ran her fingers over a few of the pouches until she found familiar gold stitches and embroidered coins against red velvet. It had belonged to Lupos Voss, a pickpocket gang leader known for operating in Gold Valley.

Voss's purse wasn't the only familiar item. Seeing red, she considered pocketing them all, but her bottomless bag was missing. Someone else must have taken it, or the warden had sold it.

Or they'd divided up some of the goods taken from the captive thieves and there were guards all over the city equipped with their possessions. She took the purse and a few other recognizable items then unfolded the soft leathers. They still smelled like the dumpster, although the stale and musty odor of the trunk clung to them too. She grimaced. Despite that one temporary flaw, it was like reuniting with an old friend.

Xavier jumped down from her neck to the edge of the chest lid. "Fondle your belongings later."

She shot him a dirty look. "Fine." He was right, and she'd have plenty of time later to marvel over those beloved pieces of her gear. After a brief accounting for each item, she stuffed the bundle into her pack.

Beneath some of the other confiscated goods, she found her weapon belt and favorite dagger along with Mira's gloves. After fastening the belt around her waist, she moved toward the door.

"Unfortunately," a man's deep voice spilled into the room from the hall, "the spymaster general doesn't see it that way and blames us for the few thieving cockroaches who got themselves killed. Shouldn't have put up the fight they did, and they wouldn't have got done in during the raids."

Rosalia slid beneath the captain's desk and squeezed her body into the tiny space.

"There's nothing to be done about it now. He wasn't in the streets with us conducting the operation, Captain. We did our best with short notice," a second man muttered. The footsteps came closer and halted nearby. She held her breath. "Strange man, that wizard."

"All wizards are a strange, devious lot. Anyway, the king and his people have gotten what they wanted out of it. The gangs are scattered to the winds, and anyone who isn't dead or bound for Heridia has already fled the city."

Heridia? The breath caught in her throat. Rosalia squeezed her eyes shut and tightened her fists. No one returned from Heridia. While on occasion, a criminal was released from the Royal Prison after repaying their debt, the inmates shipped to the colony never saw freedom again. They were shackled and confined to a destitute life of working the sugar plantations of Heridia Island instead.

"Not so many are able to flee the city now that we've finally caught those bloody smugglers. That'll be the end of their business and the start to a clean Enimura. When's that boat leave with the survivors, sir?"

They'd caught the Saladin clan too? Rosalia bit her

knuckles and suppressed a shudder, aware of Xavier's warm body against her throat. He touched the pads of his claws against her cheek in an unspoken warning—or a gesture of comfort.

"Two nights from now. There. I think those are the papers the warden required for the exchange."

The conversation drifted to another topic while one rummaged through a stack of papers on the desk. She listened to them discuss drinks at the Switch and Tap, and then the men drifted from the room.

"At least you've learned more about your friends," Xavier said. He was right against her ear, filling her hood again with the scent of wood and forest.

"Barely enough information."

"Beggars can't be choosers. A few minutes ago, you had no information at all. And now, you're armed with the most valuable weapon of all—knowledge."

17

GIFTS AND MAGIC

AFTER CLEANING AND OILING HER PREFERRED leathers, Rosalia perched on the edge of a chair in the sitting room and polished Xavier's exotic *anellan* with shade dust until the metallic gleam faded to a gentle matte black. While pretty, it shone too bright, and the best weapons were the ones a mark never saw coming.

Not that she would know, since she'd never killed anyone in all her life. Wounding a man in self-defense was one thing, but taking another life... Rosalia wasn't sure if she could do it.

And yet Xavier claimed her mother had been Queen Morwen's personal assassin.

Why hadn't Hadrian and Lacherra told her? Had they even known at all? With each discovery she made, more questions arose.

As she completed her work, Xavier stepped into the sitting parlor and set a sturdy pair of leather bracers in front of her wrapped with a loose layer of linen. A few gears shone bronze in the lantern light.

"What are these?"

A grin spread over his face, revealing several of his white teeth. She'd never noticed before how a few of them appeared a little more pronounced than others. "An invention. These are a couple things I made some time ago when I didn't specialize in clocks and engines. They were a commission for an eccentric elven lord who believed there were spies sent from Nairubia to steal into his residence and learn his secrets."

"And why doesn't he have it?"

Xavier's strong, articulate fingers took her by the wrist, and then he fastened the invention in place with a few buckles. He did the same for the other arm. The right one had the weight of a wrist bow and a few notches near her palm. "He had a lethal bout of paranoia with a relative shortly before I finished it."

"Oh. Well, shit."

He laughed. "I know. It didn't surprise me at all."

"What are they for?

"A number of things. A few of the functions still require some work and fiddling, but the main features are operative." After directing her left wrist away from them, he pressed a button she hadn't noticed on the gauntlet's palm. A hidden blade as long as her forearm sprang out. He released the button, and the knife withdrew back inside.

Rosalia gasped. "I've heard of similar inventions among the elven rangers."

"It's a practical component of their equipment, but I've added a few... alterations. Come with me and you can test them in the sewers."

Intrigued, she followed him while testing the spring-loaded blade. *Shnnnk.* It popped out with the speed of a bullet.

"Do you like it?"

"It's amazing."

He hadn't been joking about the extensive pipelines beneath Enimura. A few of the thieves had traveled them as shortcuts, but Rosalia had never been that desperate to escape the city watch that she'd wallow through filth, even if one of the gangs called it their home.

Though she *had* been desperate enough to swim through filth to escape a dragon.

Where Xavier took her, the water smelled like wet stone and plant life instead of detritus and trash. A narrow catwalk spanned above them as they crossed ankle-deep water, both ends leading into dark alcoves and different areas of the underground passage.

"There. Do you see that ledge above us?" Xavier asked.

"What about it?"

"Aim at it with your right hand and push the button beneath your thumb."

Rosalia followed his directions. Something snapped, and then she was hurtling through the air and flying toward the ledge. Her shriek echoed within the small space, but instinct took over and she grasped the ledge with both hands instead of colliding into it face-first and losing all of her teeth. As she vaulted over, the grappling hook that had dragged her to the ledge loosened from the stone.

The ride had been exhilarating and terrifying, sending her heart into a wild rhythm. She lay there for a while on her stomach until the trembling subsided, and when she glanced up, Xavier was crouched beside her with an enormous grin on his face.

"The grappling hook can penetrate most stones and grasp on to solid material. I used only the best elfsteel and added charms to increase its durability. Do you still like it?"

Rosalia considered punching him in the nose. "I'd be a fool not to," she gritted between her teeth instead. She rolled over and sat up.

He carried on, oblivious to her irritation. "The left bracer with the blade does multiple things. Here. If you curl these two fingers, you'll find a notch at the edge of the band. Press."

A dart decorated with a bright purple feather hit the wall opposite them with a subtle snap.

"It'll hold up to five darts at once and each has been laced with a powerful sedative. Reloading it on the go can be tricky—I hadn't gotten around to perfecting the design —so I wouldn't suggest unloading them all at once."

Her sore mood evaporated. The desire to break his nose was replaced by a pressing need to kiss every inch of his face instead. Propriety and her own obstinacy held the desire at bay.

She would not kiss Xavier Bane, no matter how much

sex appeal he oozed in the narrow space. Or how good he smelled. Or the gifts he gave her that rivaled anything Bonare had ever given Mira. Her heart hurt again for a second, a brief pang. Mira.

Mira would have envied her so much. He'd given her a blowgun, grappling hook, and an elfsteel sword in two flexible bracers, as if he'd taken measurements from her arm and molded it to the perfect dimensions.

Only a few days earlier, she'd envied Mira's wall-climbing gloves. Now she had a gift of her own to treasure. Her vision blurred, but the tears didn't fall. Wouldn't fall.

"Thank you for this. It means a lot to me."

"That isn't all."

"What?"

The corner of his mouth rose in another wry smile. "For my final gift to you, I present you with these." He reached into the satchel and removed a set of goggles with multiple colored lenses. "Try them on."

"What do they do?" Rosalia slipped them on then stumbled back from the bright orange and red glare. She saw Xavier and his footsteps as bold silhouettes. Even the rungs of the ladder had hints of fading color where he'd touched it to climb to her level.

"As a dragon, my night vision is enhanced, and few things can trick my sense of smell. This... well, it's something I made some time ago and believe will be of use to you in the coming days. I recently made some adjustments once I realized it could come in handy during your burglarizing endeavors."

"It's amazing."

"That one will allow you to see heat, which is ideal for detecting hidden dangers."

"Or following footsteps," she murmured.

"The lenses are also interchangeable. If you twist that knob, it'll rotate to the next view. There's a scope, and also a setting designed to enhance your vision in total darkness."

She tried those next then clapped her hands with glee.

"I brought this out of my storage to help you with the rescue tonight, since it's the only aid I'm able to give."

"Nonsense. You can come along again in your tiny dragon form."

When Xavier shook his head, a queasy feeling settled in her stomach. Did he really intend to send her out there alone to sneak her way aboard a ship manned by dozens of sailors? He may as well toss her into the brig with them.

"Why not?"

"It isn't that I don't want to accompany you, but that I'd be a liability to you. Stealth and legerdemain are not my forte. I'll slow you down."

"You didn't slow me down at all last night, and you seemed pretty damned stealthy to me."

"You don't understand, Rosalia. I can't help you because... I can't transform. Not tonight."

"*What*? What do you mean you can't transform?" She struggled to control her voice, but it cracked and rose with her growing panic.

"I can't transform," Xavier repeated. He raised his face to a grate above them and the thin slashes of starlit sky visible through it. She barely saw the silhouette of the new moon. "Three nights each moon cycle, I'm helpless. I can't transform. I can't become a dragon. I'm only a man."

Studying his grim expression confirmed his words as truth. Her hopes sank, a tight fist closing an iron grip around her heart.

During the day, her cohort had wandered down to the docks to follow up on a maintenance call to some rich baron's yacht. While there, he'd picked up tasty bits of gossip for her and determined which naval ship was soon to set sail.

The surviving thieves in captivity had to be aboard the *Noble Sword*, as it was the only military ship due to leave. Unfortunately, it was also a highly guarded military vessel with roving guards and alert sailors on every deck.

"Then they're doomed. Gregarus will have them on a ship to Heridia by dawn, and I'll never see any of them again. I failed them all."

"That isn't true. With some planning, we can still rescue your friends."

"How? I've never been aboard a naval ship, and I can't fight my way through a few dozen sailors. If I can't safely get on the ship, how can I get anyone off with me without getting all of us killed?"

Xavier stroked his chin. "I've worked on a number of

the new naval cruisers. The *Noble Sword* is definitely a new ship."

A flicker of hope welled in her chest. "And many of the new ships are identical in design. Are you able to draw a map?"

"Of course."

They returned to the hoard and entered his study where Xavier sketched out what he remembered of the ship's interior. "The main deck is where you'll come in. There's no other way to access the rest of the ship, you see. And the brig is down below in the deepest part of the ship. It'll be here, aft of the armory."

"What the hell is aft?"

He sketched another room. "Behind. About here. I only recall as much because I'd been curious about the differences between a Saudonian naval ship and an Ilyrian naval ship. One of the sailors enjoyed watching me repair the engine and gave me a tour. There were two of them armed here in the cargo deck on the lowest level of the ship's belly." He drew an X over the armory. "Above that, there's the gun deck and berth where the sailors rest when they're off duty."

"The moment we try to leave the ship, they'll see us. The *Noble Sword* is my friend Adriano's old ship, and it's enormous."

"It is, but I also know they're anchored, and when a ship is anchored at port, most of the sailors are released to shore leave. Most won't return until a few hours before dawn if they're expected to set sail at sunrise."

He just had all the answers, didn't he? She resented

him for a moment, loathing he couldn't go with her until she swallowed back her irritation. It wasn't his fault. This was hers, and now she'd risk her life to right it.

"All right. I'll go change, then."

Rosalia left Xavier behind in the sitting room. The bedroom he'd given her was spacious and as large as all four rooms of the suite she'd rented with Mira. The best part was the porcelain tub in the corner and the endless amount of hot water that steamed from the spigot.

Her leathers occupied a borrowed stand from the armory, newly conditioned and then dusted until the gleam vanished entirely. After exchanging her borrowed tunic and leggings for thief's garb, she wondered how Xavier could have so much faith in her.

She sat on the bedside and stared at her own hands. For all her gifts and magic, what good had any of it done her when she needed it to work the most? She'd let down her only family, the people who had pulled her off the streets and brought her into their fold without question.

And if she didn't get off her ass, she'd never avenge Frederico. Swallowing the bitter taste in her mouth, she closed her eyes and tried to feel that spark of magic Xavier claimed she had. Somewhere deep inside, the ability was waiting to ignite.

"Rosalia?"

Her eyes snapped open. Xavier watched her from the open doorway, one hand against the stone frame. "Yes?

"Are you all right?"

"No."

He stepped inside. "Would you like to talk about it?"

"No. Not really. I mean... yes. I would. I was thinking about how I've let everyone down."

Xavier sat beside her, his weight shifting the mattress beneath them. "That isn't true, Rosa." His warm palm settled over her knuckles. "You haven't let anyone down yet, because the boat is still there. And who are you?"

"A fraud."

"No. You are the best thief in all of Enimura."

"Only because everyone else is dead."

"You were before then as well. Otherwise, Hadrian wouldn't have tasked *you* with finding the mirror. Are you telling me the best thief this city has ever seen can't create a scheme to smuggle her friends off a ship?"

"You have too much faith in me."

"I have faith in a woman who broke through three layers of magical enchantments and the best clockwork mechanisms I've created in decades. You performed a miraculous feat by putting your mind to it."

"Xavier, it wasn't skill that night. It was luck. I didn't know the first thing I was doing."

He touched her chin and raised her face to make eye contact with him, strong fingers curving over the lower edge of her jaw. "The blood of your mother runs through your veins. She was a djinn, and that means something. She had the power to bend reality and to make things happen in her favor. But the best part about her wasn't her magic—it was her strength and willingness to use those powers to do amazing things in the service of Queen Morwen. Especially when she stole this mirror from the royal family and gave it to me to protect."

"But I'm not her. I could never be her." She blinked a few times until the stinging faded, too stubborn to cry anymore tears. "I don't understand my gift. I don't even know if I have one at all."

Xavier dried her cheek with his thumb. "Then discover it and learn to understand it. You have one chance, and then the last people you love in this world are going to be gone. Everyone who hasn't been taken by death will be aboard a ship bound for hard slave labor."

18

THE IMPOSSIBLE

ROSALIA CROUCHED IN THE SHADOWS OF THE DOCKS. She twisted one of the knobs on her goggles to activate the enhanced heat vision feature and stared at the myriad of warm colors.

In the belly of the ship, a vague and indefinable crimson glow told her there were many people down below near the cargo hold. That was where her friends and fellow thieves would be held until they were taken away to the island penal colony to work long and difficult lives harvesting sugar cane.

For the past fifteen minutes, two patrolmen had made the rounds on the deck, one occasionally wandering down the gangplank onto the pier where he'd bullshit with another man. They both held lanterns. Rosalia saw two more stationary alchemical lamps casting overlapping pools of light on the main deck near the starboard rail. The quarterdeck and forecastle each had another lamp of their own.

A week ago, she'd have said it was impossible.

Now it was merely necessary.

I can do this.

She moved closer and knelt behind an empty crate. Soon after, the man on the pier turned his back to her and faced the open sea.

Then he unfastened his britches.

Rosalia grimaced and scurried past him, praying he didn't perceive more than a dark shadow against the wooden path. Seconds later, deck planks were beneath her soft leather boots and the boisterous laughter of crewmen spilled from the open hatch. She lurked in the shadows of the main deck, keeping to portside, and listened until the noise subsided. Boots creaked against wood, and one of the patrolling sailors stepped onto the quarterdeck with his back to her. The other disappeared into the hatch leading to the gun deck, his soles thumping against a set of stairs so steep they resembled a ladder.

She waited a few beats then followed with light-footed grace. He disappeared down a narrow corridor and vanished from sight, taking his lantern with him. Good.

According to Xavier's map, she'd find the brig in the lowest level of the ship near the cargo hold. She made her way along, scurrying into the shadows and wedging her body into a small nook between the wall and two barrels of fresh produce when another sailor passed by. He nabbed an apple off the top, oblivious to the thief tucked between them, and continued down the passage.

The moment he was gone, she descended to the next

level via another hatch and slipped by two armed men until she encountered an alert pair of sailors guarding the brig.

At least four cells made up the ship's small jail, and they were all overcrowded with manacled prisoners.

"Shut up over there before I give you filthy thieves something to really bitch about."

"Come in here and say it to my face," a man snarled.

"You need someone to work you over again? Fine. Let's go, tough guy."

Rosalia raised the wrist bow and tucked the tip of her index and middle fingers toward the concealed button beside her palm. The dart landed in the guard's meaty posterior, and he jumped a mile high. He clapped a hand to his bottom and spun off balance into the crates behind him before crashing into the floor. She fired again, striking the second guard in the thigh. He jerked and stumbled against the bulkhead. His head bounced off it with a satisfying thud when he fell, pulled under by the tranquilizer in less than three seconds flat.

Perfect.

A few prisoners near the bars jumped up. "What in the hell was that?" a gruff voice demanded.

"Don't sound good, whatever it was. Can you see anything?"

"Not a damned thing," a familiar, much younger voice replied.

Rosalia stepped up to the bars and gazed into Jabari's dirty face. Gods, she wanted to hug him and whisk him away from the danger. The assholes had shoved him behind bars with a dozen other men and one of them wasn't moving. "Shh. It's me. Don't make any noise."

"Rosalia?" Jabari squinted at her in the dark through his left eye. The other had swollen shut, dark purple to match his other bruises. "I must be dreaming. The guards at the jail said you were dead. Said a dragon had roasted you on the way to your execution."

"Faked," she whispered back. "I came to rescue all of you."

"There's no rescuing us. There's guards all over, and they come down here too often. Haven't eaten since before we were all held overnight in the jail, and don't suspect we will anytime soon. We're bound for the penal colony on Heridia. They mean to break us before we arrive. Have us desperate to work the rest of our lives for crumbs."

"I know."

"Then get out now while you've got the chance. Save yourself."

"No. I *will* rescue you. Do any of you know how to sail a ship? Does anyone understand how to get this thing moving?"

An older man moved up to the bars and grasped them with weathered, brown hands. It took her a few moments to recognize the smuggler's creased and wrinkled face. He and his men had always smuggled in casks of elven wine to Hadrian, bringing it over from Ilyria for the bar without paying the heavy tariffs and taxes the king had affixed to anything foreign.

Alberto Saladin's mouth spread into a crooked grin.

"I can. Got some of my crew here with me. It'll be an easy job." He gestured to Sergio and Horatio, two brothers tasked with the heavy lifting during smuggling runs, and his first mate Durum. "The four of us do an occasional bit of work on ships like this during the days—you know, our honest work—but I understand how these newfangled ships operate. This one's got one of those engines in her belly not too far from where we are now. It will have to be fed and primed before we can sail."

Rosalia glanced over the other two cells in the brig and knelt before the lock with her pickset. "Then we better get moving. Who's able to fight?"

"If it means freedom, we're all able to fuckin' fight," Alberto said.

"My knees may be broken," a man said from where he lay on the floor of the filthy cell, "but you give me a shank and I'll crawl to gut one of these pigs."

Most of them were battered and injured, the only two women among them in equally poor shape. Injured fighters were better than no fighters, and if the careful plan she'd designed with Xavier worked, there wouldn't be a need for any bloodshed at all.

The door swung open, an easy lock. "If you have chains, then you have weapons. They can be used to bludgeon and choke the unaware if you're silent. Both guards I took down were armed with a long sword. Who's capable with a blade?"

"I am," Sergio said. "But you know that."

After he spoke up, a slim woman stepped forward to the bars. She was taller than Rosalia, and her scarred arms had the definition of a fighter. Her nose had recently been broken, and both eyes were shadowed by purple. The symmetry of her face was off, one jaw bruised and swollen. "I'm good with a saber."

Another man squeezed his way to the front, looking lean and hard, dark hair around his shoulders and narrow, pointed face. "So am I." Recognition flit across her mind until she remembered him from the scene in Vermeil. He'd been the mysterious swordsman protecting the carriage. "Soraya and I worked for Marcolo Aleppo. She guarded his second-in-command. I'm Luca."

"I thought you were familiar. You both look injured though."

"They softened us a little," Soraya said, "but it only makes me thirstier for blood."

Aleppo didn't hire cheap labor or incapable fighters. That they had survived the attack meant fate was in her favor.

"That's all I need to know." Rosalia freed them from the chains, delighted by how easily the locks yielded to her skill with Xavier's pickset. She'd barely touched the pins. "You two come with me. Sergio and Horacio, you take the swords and protect our rear. If we can get into the armory, that'll be weapons for everyone."

"What about the rest of us?"

Rosalia tossed her spare picks to Jabari and passed him a stiletto. She kept Xavier's charmed tools for herself. "Remember what I taught you about locks and release the others. I brought something to incapacitate the sailors in the sleeping quarters. Otherwise, we don't have a chance of making it out of this. Everybody must be mobile if a fight begins."

Jabari hurried to work. "Got it."

With a small group behind her, Rosalia led the way from the brig and into the naval ship's unfamiliar passageways. The spy eyes came in handy again when she pulled them down over her face. She looked up a level, saw many immobile silhouettes of men on the deck above them, no doubt sleeping after a long day of work on the main deck. There were only two shapes ahead of them, and one in the distance near the ship's storeroom.

One of the guards stretched and yawned. "Gonna go step into the mess for a second. I'm damned hungry."

"And just leave me here all alone?"

The other snorted. "What do you expect to happen at the second hour of night?"

They fussed at each other for a moment, and then one ambled off after promising to return with a pint for his friend. Drinking on the job. She shook her head and moistened her lips. Anticipation tingled down to the tips of her fingers.

The ease in which she'd infiltrated the ship made her wonder if Xavier was right about her gift. Everything had fallen into place, the plan flawless down to the last detail. All her life, she'd wondered if the twins of Fate and Fortune lit her path to success.

Maybe she'd made her own luck, after all.

Banking on that, she raised her wrist and fired. Her third dart sank into the lone sailor's well-formed posterior, and then he slumped to the floor senselessly. He didn't even squeak.

"That's good shit, whatever you've got," Soraya murmured. She liberated the unfortunate guard of his sabers and passed one to Luca. He grinned and dipped into a bow with an exaggerated flourish.

While they dragged the guard out of sight, Rosalia crouched in front of the armory door. "It helps when you have access to rare and difficult-to-find reagents." And a filthy rich dragon at your disposal.

Three complicated padlocks and a bar stood between them and the weaponry. The charmed picks wiggled pins and tumblers out of her way, and then the heavy door swung outward, revealing a bounty of longbows, pistols, cutlasses, and gear meant for defending against boarding parties.

Satisfied, she straightened and glanced at the group. "Arm yourselves and everyone else in the cells. We don't have much time before he's back."

"What do you want us to do after that?"

"We take prisoners for now. Kill no one unless it's absolutely necessary. There's plenty of rope in the store-room for that. You'll encounter one man along the way to the engines, but I want you to bind him. Now pass the message along."

Luca nodded. "We will."

If her knowledge of naval life was correct after many years of listening to Adriano's tales, most of the crew would be ashore enjoying the rest of their leave and spending time with their families. They wouldn't report in for duty to set sail until a few hours before dawn.

Xavier was right. The ship's at half the usual staffing, a mere skeleton crew until morning. We can do this. We have the advantage.

She slid her spy eyes on again. Counting the number of shapes in the berth allayed her worries. Less than two dozen. That'd be several men out of the fight and drugged so heavily they couldn't lift their heads from their pillows. Or the floor, depending on where they fell.

Rosalia had never led a gang of thieves before, but she'd accompanied Hadrian on complicated heists requiring more than one body in the past. She'd loathed those, wondering how he withstood the pressure of being responsible for so many people.

After signaling for the others to linger down below, she went up the hatch first and crouched before making her way into position beside a barrel on the berthing deck. Awareness was low, not a guard in sight.

The sailors all slept on cots and hammocks, most oblivious. Four men played a quiet game of cards in the corner.

"Can't believe they're putting us back out there when we've only been at port for a bloody week," one of them grumbled from his hammock. He tapped the ashes from a clove cigarette onto a dish below him. "Of all the ships to volunteer for this shit..."

"Rather be at home shagging the missus myself, but what can you do? It's money in our purses at least."

Rosalia tugged the plug from the knock-out grenade,

wincing at the little pop and a subtle hiss it made. She rolled it underhand across the floor then dropped through the hatch again. Xavier had sworn he treated her mask's lining with a special antidote guaranteed to neutralize the potion's effects, but she preferred not to test it.

"The hell's that?"

"Something smells... sorta... funny."

A chorus of concerned voices reached her ears, followed by a few muted thumps as bodies toppled to the deck. Damn. If Xavier's calculations could be trusted, they'd have to wait a full minute before the deck was safe.

A series of noisy thumps thundered above their heads, punctuated by a loud thump, then silence. More sailors arrived from other parts of the ship, no doubt alarmed by the noise, and one by one, they succumbed, too, until the mist cleared.

Luca appeared behind her, brows squeezed together. "What was that?"

"Knock-out potion in a rapid diffusing sphere. Kinda had a friend alter the design of a Shade Out bomb for me."

"Excellent. I like how you work."

"I saved that for their dormitory since the darts are limited. I only have two left now, but that took out nearly two dozen of them at once."

The odds remained in their favor thus far. Within minutes of putting her plan into action, she'd managed to incapacitate most of the ship without a single loss of life.

Good. Thieves weren't the same as murderers, although one gang—the Night Vipers—had been partial to accepting assassination contracts on behalf of the gentry and nobility on occasion. If it meant keeping their own hands clean, rich and wealthy clientele happily paid for their poorer adversaries and competition to be eliminated. Those contracts were rare and monitored closely.

What would they do without the Vipers? she wondered. Their operation had been a terrifying but integral part of Enimura tradition going back since the founding of the three guilds. At one point, Hadrian mentioned Grandmaster Ombre bringing all of the gang leaders together to discuss talk of instituting a fourth guild for assassination, the first of its kind across the eleven kingdoms.

Rosalia climbed up the hatch to the upper level. The fog dispersed, and the faint hint of night-blooming jasmine faded. "All right," she whispered down to the others. One by one, the able-bodied thieves came after her.

There was no turning back now.

———

By the time the escaped thieves secured the living area and Rosalia made it to the top deck, the battle was winding down with minimal bloodshed and only a single casualty. There had only been a few men spread throughout the berth and gun deck, and fewer patrolling topside.

One of the older thieves had been slashed, cut down brutally during the uprising against the small number of trained naval crew on the main deck. Luca and Soraya had the rest well in hand, the former as deadly barefoot and in rags as he'd been the night Rosalia watched him take down a half dozen city watchman to protect his employer.

Alberto controlled the wheel while Durum and Horatio secured the quarterdeck. They had already disabled the handful of sailors there. The naval ship pulled from the harbor, and in the distance, dozens of armed sailors rushed down the docks, pursued by city watchmen aiming bows and nocking arrows. No sooner did her magnified lenses focus on the figure leading them, did a sense of dread spread through the pit of her stomach and turn her confidence to ice.

Adriano. Not once had she expected to encounter him during their little coup, hoping he'd be at home mourning her, too grief stricken to resume any of his duties.

Wishful thinking maybe.

"Don't fire! Everyone down!" Rosalia cried. Her hood flew off as she thrust Jabari to the deck beneath her and crouched above him, protecting the boy from the volley of arrows falling all around them. One pierced one of their captives in the arm, but at first glance it appeared superficial. Another struck a fellow thief in the thigh. He stumbled and collapsed.

With an anguished cry, Pachenzo raised his bow and aimed. The arrow could have been destined for anyone—a sailor, a watchman, or her best childhood friend.

"No!" Rosalia lunged at Pachenzo and tackled him to the deck. The shot went wide, missing Adriano by a mile.

Blessed Light of Arcadian. That had been meant for her friend after all, and had she been a split second later, the fletching would be protruding from his chest.

"The hell you go and do that for? Ain't nothing but a fucking pig in white."

"Enough lives have been lost."

When she glanced at the pier, Adriano stood at the end of it, staring at the ship with wide eyes.

Damn. Had he recognized her? *Could* he recognize her at this distance? If anyone knew her preferred garb while on the job, it would be him.

"Get off me!"

Pachenzo shoved her off and swept the bow from the deck again. He was determined, a fury in him that nocked the arrow a second time until she ejected the blade from her bracer and slashed the string.

"No! We won't harm them. It isn't necessary to spill anymore blood than what's already stained this deck. We've taken the ship, and that's what matters most when it comes to my plan."

Luca had his heel on the neck of a sailor. He glanced at her and raised one dark brow. "What do you say we do with them then?"

"We'll toss them into the longboat and let them paddle back to Enimura once we've gained distance. Perhaps the beach guard will find them first, all the better to distract them from coming after us."

Pachenzo growled. "What reason we got for listening

to you? You ain't did shit but open a door. Hell, given some time, one of us may have managed that ourselves."

Jabari charged forward across the wooden deck on bare feet with both fists clenched at his sides. Resentment and anger contorted his youthful but swollen face. "Hey! You can't speak to Rosalia that way! She did more than just free us. She saved our lives, and you owe her an apology."

"No one asked you, kid. Beat it while grown folk are talking."

The ship drifted farther from the harbor, moving from the mouth of the bay and approaching the open sea with increasing speed. They had a head start and the night in their favor, none of the other ships prepared or manned to suddenly withdraw from dock and pursue them.

Rosalia's heart pounded in her chest. The others had gone silent, but Soraya's fingers tightened over her sword hilt. Luca stepped closer to her. A brief, curt nod exchanged between them as the two appeared to communicate in body language.

They were either on her side or plotting to throw her overboard.

"This is our chance to raise the black flag and go off to do whatever we want. We have a naval ship stocked for a voyage, armed with guns, and loaded with ammo." Pachenzo slammed a fist into his palm. "We have everything we need to take the seas, and we may never have this kind of opportunity again. Imagine the power below us in that gun berth. Look at the weapons we've taken from the armory. Outfitted and equipped like this, nothing can stop us."

Luca stared at Pachenzo a moment. Then he cracked an uneven grin and turned away to laugh.

Soraya gave a throaty chuckle. "That's your big plan? You don't even know what she plans to do, and you're already dismissing her idea in favor of yours?"

"It can't be as good as getting rich looting ships. Thievin' is what we know," a former prisoner said. "Let's hear him out. He's been on a pirate ship before."

A low murmur of agreement spread over the group.

Sergio tossed back his head, his thunderous laughter echoing across the midnight sky. "So have I, and I can tell you it's nothing great. A lot of difficult work and struggle, hungry days when there are no ships in sight, and loss of lives when you encounter the wrong one. They don't all wear their protection where you can see them either. It's a difficult job discerning the weak from the strong, but you make one fuck up and everyone's a goner."

Horatio nodded. "He speaks the truth. A meek merchant vessel may appear to be a kitten until her claws come out and you realize you've caught a tiger. You haven't faced a struggle until you watch a pair of battlemages emerge from below deck with their spell books armed and ready. You thought those city watchmen kicked your asses before slinging you in a cell? Battlemages are merciless." He shook his head.

A few voices quieted. "Battlemages?" someone asked.

"Aye. Battlemages raining lightning and fire down on your sails like there's no tomorrow. And somehow, I'm here to tell the tale and warn you about it. Barely got out of that scrape by the skin of our fucking teeth. They'll incinerate you and sweep your cinders off the deck without thinking twice."

"Still, they can't all afford to hire magicians," a younger thief spoke up. "Right, Pachenzo?"

"Right. Those odds are small, only the wealthiest merchants can afford that kind of aid. I say we take our chance as pirates with odds no different than if we were to continue a life of theft. She ain't told us nothing that convinces me we should be followin' her orders."

"We want to take our chances as pirates. There are fat merchant ships out there on the waves. I've seen them!" another thief shouted.

Pachenzo puffed his chest out. "Y'see? No one cares about her plan. She's just a child, and she ain't no boss of me."

"*I* say she's the boss." Moving stiffly on his damaged leg, Alberto descended the steps from the quarterdeck and strode up to them, clutching a broomstick for a cane. "Who knows how to sail? They say you've been on a ship, but do you know how to *sail*? You learn anything about that while you was out there on the sea?"

Pachenzo said nothing.

"I expected as much. The two of us"—Alberto pointed at him and Durum—"are all you have capable of operating this ship. The way I see it, you need us, otherwise you've got a pretty piece of wood and steel as likely to capsize as it is to deliver you to a life of piracy."

Durum grunted.

"Rosalia went through a lot of trouble, at great personal peril to herself, and I ain't about to let you chuckleheads fuck it up for all of us. Now I say we hear her out."

Luca nodded. "As do I. She's earned our loyalty until she proves it's undeserved. Anyone disagree with me—"

"Or me," Soraya said.

"—can swim back ashore."

The dissenters quieted.

Luca grinned. "Excellent. Glad we are able to all see eye to eye here."

"As am I," Sergio said, while Horatio nodded alongside him. "It would have been quite unfortunate for anyone to tumble overboard with their manacles restored in place."

Alberto crossed his arms over his barrel chest. "We have no need for the longboats, and since we've already acquired a free naval ship, we can toss 'em in with a single oar and leave them to their luck. Listen to the woman. She got us this far, and she deserves our respect. We're thieves, not assholes."

"Speak for yourself," Horatio said.

A couple of the them chuckled.

As a low murmur of discussion went over the crowd of former prisoners, her gaze darted to the group, and she only relaxed when their heads began to nod.

Pachenzo's shoulders dropped. "I hope you're right about this."

An hour later, enough distance spanned between the *Sword* and port that Alberto permitted them to load the longboats and set them down on the waves. As promised, the sailors received a single oar, though most of them were still unconscious, their drowsy heads lolling left and right.

That was one less responsibility on Rosalia's plate. Now she just had to hope her motley crew were up for the task of sailing to Ilyria.

19

_____

DESTINY

It took Rosalia most of the night and the next morning before the crew drove her to wondering if execution would have been better. Of the twenty-six former prisoners, nine had been beaten too cruelly to provide help, and almost half of the remaining thieves resented taking orders from her. Alberto tried to help, but it wasn't until Luca and Soraya stepped forward and doubled down on their vow to throw any dissenters into the sea, that there was finally peace.

Between her and the seasoned smuggler, they managed to assign jobs and somehow keep the ship afloat on the turbulent seas. The injured were given simple tasks to complete below deck, making meals in the galley, or sitting on stools and crates while chopping vegetables to rest their battered or broken limbs.

"Gods, they sure took their pleasure in beating inmates bound for the slave port. How were you all to work when they've laid you up in your cells?" Rosalia asked, popping into the room where the ship kept its small number of livestock.

The young thief milking one of the ship's three goats grimaced. Even the youngest thief taken alive hadn't been exempt from physical abuse. Enrikos had a bruised face and a busted lip, his right arm in a makeshift sling. He couldn't have been more than seven or eight and had been one of her favorite urchins to contract when she needed a little surveillance on a mark. He was also a lieutenant among the Sewer Rats, a gang run almost entirely by kids. "They'd have found other ways to make use of us, just as you have. Uh, not that I mind. Milking goats and getting pecked by chickens ain't as bad as slave labor or staying in the workhouses, and all that. You don't listen to the ones bitching and moaning, Rosalia."

She smiled at him. "I didn't intend to listen to them. Though I suspect Luca is tired of their complaints and may make good on his threat to throw someone overboard."

"That wasn't a threat. That was a promise. I've seen him in action before for Aleppo."

"Yeah?"

"He nearly gutted a man once. Wasn't supposed to see it, I don't think. He'd brought the poor asshole down into the sewers for a bit of private hide-the-knife time, you know? And I was down there minding my own business when he came down with Soraya and two other guys who worked for the big boss. Next thing I know, there's blood everywhere. The other two quieted up nice and proper, said they'd make good on their overdue payments to Aleppo and give no more problems."

"So he made an example of one?"

Enrikos nodded. "That's how those types get everybody to mind the big bosses. I don't think he died either, cause his two friends picked him up and carried him off after that. He was still groaning."

"Yeah. A dead thief can't pay his taxes to the boss. And if he's undercut the boss, he sure can't repay that with interest if he's fish food."

Murder was out of the question when it came to the Thieves Guild, but the leaders like Hadrian and Aleppo had their ways of gaining obedience, otherwise they wouldn't be the boss and disorganization would corrupt the complicated infrastructure that kept the guild running like a well-oiled clockwork machine.

At least it had been running like one until King Gregarus decided to say to bash it all to hell.

"Hey, Rosalia?"

"Hm?"

"Thanks. For rescuing us. We appreciate it, you know."

She smiled down at the kid and mussed his curly hair. "No need to thank me."

"I know. Some of the others won't say it 'cause they're too busy acting like jackasses, but I figure the rest of us can at least show we're grateful."

Rosalia scooped a bucket from a barrel of grain and wandered around the livestock quarters, scattering handfuls over the ground for the clucking chickens.

"What's going to happen to all of us now? Alberto says we're heading to Ilyria. I thought all elves hated Saudonians."

"We are, and they don't. The elves despise our kingdom's leadership and our allies, with good reason as we've recently learned."

"True."

"Anyway, we haven't many other places to go. An acquaintance told me to get us sailing to Ilyria, and that he'd put word in with their coastguard announcing us as refugees."

"Do you trust him?"

She pursed her lips and considered it. Xavier had saved her from certain death, sheltered her, and given her all the tools required to rescue two dozen more lives. Trust was putting it mildly, even if there were times she wanted to physically correct his arrogance with a sharp punch to the nose.

"Yes. He's a good man. I'd trust him with my life. He'll do right by us."

The child's dark eyes shone with hope.

"I'll take these up to the galley for you."

After delivering a few dozen eggs to the galley, she spent the rest of the day assisting with other menial tasks around the ship, clueless about sailing but capable of taking orders from Alberto and Sergio. Then she slept on a hammock in the berth. There were only three officers' cabins on the naval ship—captain's, lieutenant's, and physician's quarters—and they'd given those beds to the thieves with assorted serious injuries, a couple folk with internal injuries, and a guy with shattered knees.

The next day wasn't any better, although she spent her time alternating between learning the cast nets and loading the guns. Alberto wanted any of the able-bodied crew to know how to arm the cannons if the Saudonian King's Navy caught them.

Despite all their preparation, her greatest hope was that the training wouldn't be needed at all, and that the goddess of the sea safely swept her newfound gang into the welcoming arms of the elves.

Please, Nindar, guide us to where we belong.

———

ROSALIA HAD BEEN in the crow's nest as the lookout since sunrise, distrusting anyone else to watch for naval ships on the horizon. It was the evening of their third day at sea, and the sun had already made her miserable, seeming hotter when it reflected off the white-capped waves than it had been in the desert.

Jabari climbed up beside her. "Take a break, Rosalia. I've got this for a while. Which way am I looking?"

"West. Actually no, they'll be sailing from south, south west. Alberto says there's a great current coming in, and he thinks they'll be sailing on it if they want any chance of attempting to overtake us."

"Okay. What else do I need to know?"

She passed the telescope into his hands. "That's it. Just keep an eye on the horizon for ships from Saudonia.

It's very, very important for us to know right away if they've discovered us. All right?"

Wearing a stern expression on his youthful face, lips pressed thin and brow squished close, the young boy nodded. "All right. You and Alberto can count on me."

True to his word, Alberto's knowledge of the sea had put enough distance between them and Enimura's port that the likelihood of discovery was small indeed, especially now that the crew had entered contested waters. She'd listened to Adriano bitch and moan enough about harmless skirmishes between the two kingdoms.

Please, let Xavier be right about the elves. There were still some days ahead before they even encountered land, the elven shores hundreds of miles from Saudonia's coastline.

After leaving Jabari in the crow's nest as their lookout, she made a pit stop on the quarter deck to check in with Alberto.

He gave her a dubious glance when she approached. "Are you sure you want us to head to Ilyria? I might have a couple contacts or two willing to shelter some of us, but I doubt the elves will be willing to take in an entire boatload of thieves. Hell, I never come this way unless we're picking up silks and a few casks of their floral red." Alberto grinned, a twinkle in his gray eyes. "Speaking of good drink, you look as if you could use some. Fetch something from that barrel of rainwater over yonder before you pass out on my deck."

Too many hours in the crow's nest beneath the sweltering sun had tightened her skin and left her feeling off kilter. Woozy. She took his advice and scooped a cool cup of water from the barrel before soaking it up with a rag from her belt. Draping it over the back of her neck felt amazing, even if water dripped freely down her spine.

"Positive. It's where my cohort requested for me to lead you all to safety. Ilyria and Saudonia aren't on the best of terms right now, and my friend swore they'd accept us as refugees once he delivered a message."

"And who's this cohort? One of us who ain't been hauled in on phony charges or murdered? Who else escaped the Purge? Is it Mira?"

Her heart hurt. She shook her head and forced a wan smile. "No one you'd recognize. *He* isn't a thief, Alberto."

The old man scratched the white scruff on his chin. "Can he be trusted?"

"Absolutely."

"Hey, Rosalia!" Jabari leaned down and shouted from the crow's nest. "I see elven canvas up ahead! I thought you said we weren't going to cross them until tomorrow evening?"

Panic stiffened her spine. Could these elves be unaware of their intention to declare themselves refugees, a patrol ship prepared to punish the foreign presence daring to trespass within a few hundred miles of Ilyrian shores?

"What? Are you sure?"

"Pretty sure. I see an elven ship approaching. Wait, scratch that. *Three* elven ships!"

She hurried up the mast again and grabbed the scope from Jabari's hands.

True to his promise to help her, Xavier stood on the distant ship's deck. Her heart did a little flip in her chest. He'd done more than keep his promise. He'd brought the elves to them instead.

But how in the world had he done it when she'd left him behind in Saudonia and he was unable to fly?

Elven sailors in pristine military uniforms rushed across the deck, moving at the command of a captain at the helm. Fascinated, Rosalia watched the nose of the ship veer left and approach at greater speed. It flew across the waves faster than any Saudonian ship, despite lacking an apparent engine and relying on the wind.

"Are they friendly?" the old captain asked.

"It's my friend!"

A short while later, as the sun kissed the horizon and set the sea ablaze with streaks of golden fire, the elves reached the *Noble Sword* and dropped anchor. The crew were all a handsome and fit variety, skin tones ranging from fair and porcelain to toasted walnut, but Xavier stood out among them as different. His hair glittered like rainbow merged with shadows, and he towered at least a head taller than the largest of them, his broad shoulders more muscled compared to their lean physiques.

Seeing them all side by side, she wondered how anyone had ever confused him as one of their kind.

An elf slid a gangplank into place, connecting their portside bows, and then the captain strode over, a slim fellow with a regal posture, clothed in a long coat of white with numerous silver, green, and golden ribbons across his medal-decorated chest. The ocean breeze kicked up a few strands of the glorious mane of dark silver hair flowing over his shoulders.

"I am Captain Elurin of the *Opal Destiny*. Who's in charge?"

When no one spoke up, Rosalia cleared her throat and stepped forward. "I am."

The elf offered a hand, startling her with the benevolence in his charming smile. Instead of a brisk shake, he bowed and raised her knuckles to his lips. "Our mutual friend tells us that you and your people have suffered greatly while imprisoned in Enimura. Does anyone require medical attention?"

Rosalia nodded. "Many of my people were abused and beaten. There are a few fractured bones and some infected wounds."

Elurin glanced over his shoulder and made an unfamiliar gesture to his crew. Two elves crossed over to the *Noble Sword*, both carrying bulging leather pouches. "Take them to your injured. Have your people eaten well?"

"We have stores and a working galley. The meals have been... decent."

He inclined his head to her. "Then we will provide better. Any friend of Zaviriel is a friend of ours."

Zaviriel? Her gaze darted to Xavier. He hadn't moved from the other ship's deck and watched the exchange with a neutral expression, features stony and unreadable.

"Now, I would be honored if you would join us aboard the *Destiny*. We'll do our very best to accommodate the needs of your people during this trying time."

"I shouldn't leave them."

"Nonsense. Several members of my crew will remain aboard to lend a helping hand. I'd like to hear more about the recent changes in Enimura that led to this revolt."

He led the way onto the *Opal Destiny* and to the captain's quarters—at least, what she suspected were the captain's quarters. The polished wood floors were decorated with silk carpets while the glossy wooden walls shone beneath tapestries depicting colorful elven summers in pastel shades of gold, rose, teal, and lilac. The rich and earthy smell of a forest surrounded her all at once, setting her heart at ease even after the door shut behind them.

Yet she'd never visited a forest before in all of her life to recognize the smell, raised in a coastal desert town and surrounded by the sea, hot sand, whale oil, and salt. At least, she didn't recall ever visiting one even as a child, despite the aroma tugging at her memories and stirring a sense of peace inside her.

They settled at a table large enough to seat six people or more. An emerald, gold, and silver runner spanned the length of it, accompanied by a tea service for four beside two large bowls of elvish fruits and vegetables.

Xavier studied her from across the table. "I already apprised Elurin of the circumstances surrounding our recent acquaintance to the best of my ability, but you'll have to fill in any holes we haven't discussed, as well as the details of your escape from Enimura's harbor."

Elurin served them both with the grace of a trained host from one of the Rosewater District's fancy teahouses, though Rosalia suspected he would have put those ladies to shame. If Xavier hadn't proven men could be truly beautiful, Elurin would have convinced her in his stead.

"All right. So, it began on the evening my thiefmaster called me to take this job."

Deciding no detail was too private, she told the elf everything she'd shared with Xavier and more, including the way their client had pressed Hadrian to produce results. At the time, the buyer's impatience hadn't seemed too strange to her, but in hindsight it set off every alarm.

"I see. And of course, you stole it out from beneath this sleeping giant and made your getaway. However did you manage to give him the slip for so long?"

"Whale oil," she murmured. "It's a trick Mira and I favored, along with a few other burglars. The smell of it is often in the air in Enimura, so if you mix it with a bit of musk and shade dust, you smell like... the city itself and no hound or creature can track you."

"Quite brilliant if it was able to fool a dragon."

"It wouldn't fool me again," Xavier muttered.

One of the elvish healers popped in to report the progress among the injured thieves. Moments later, another crew member arrived with supper while Rosalia recounted their wild escape from Enimura, commandeering the *Noble Sword*, and their struggles to keep two dozen thieves from committing a mutiny.

Elurin barked out a hard laugh. He leaned back in his seat and crossed one ankle over his knee, appearing more relaxed by the moment. "Piracy. From what Juniae told me just now of your injured thieves, they wouldn't have survived boarding the weakest, least prepared merchant ship."

"Thankfully, a few of the guys aboard had the experience to deter them. And, uh, there's two really good enforcers who would have messed them up if they tried, I think. So, that's it. We're here now, and we're at the mercy of the elves."

Elurin shook his head. "Anyone with common sense knows it's impossible to remove all crime. That is why the Thieves Guild exists. Better to monitor it than to have them running wild with no rules whatsoever. When news reached us via Zaviriel of King Gregarus destroying the Enimuran chapter, our esteemed ruler chose to act in the best interest of preserving the balance. Ilyria will shelter your friends. We've already contacted Grandmaster Nemuria, and she's agreed to accept anyone who wishes to continue the life in our lands—"

"That is kind of her."

"—if they are able to follow her rules. She's strict, so time will only tell if your friends regret our meddling."

"Trust me. They won't. Anything is better than what was planned for them on Heridia."

Xavier rose from his seat. "We shouldn't keep Elurin away from his duties. I'm sure he has a lot of captaining and other things to do."

"Actually, I was enjoying the conversation and willing to leave the welfare of the *Destiny* in my lieutenant's capable hands for a while longer."

Xavier raised a brow. "Any excuse to skive off from a little work, eh?"

Rosalia's brows popped up as she observed the friendly banter between the two men. They were grinning, but something about Xavier's smile didn't reach his eyes. Forced.

"What good is there in having a title like captain if I don't enjoy delegating a few tasks every now and then?"

"Just the same. I'm sure she's exhausted after three days of babysitting her peers. C'mon. I'll let you bunk with me."

Rosalia considered her hammock in the berth. "Maybe I'd rather go back to the *Sword*. My friends are there, and everyone is probably a little nervous with elves crawling all over and taking charge."

"I'll head over and have a word with them," Elurin volunteered. He led them to the cabin door. "While the greater news is yours to share, I'd like to meet this Alberto and Sergio if they're the ones responsible for sailing that ungainly thing to us with a mere skeleton crew of untrained men. Perhaps there's a place for them among the Ilyrian Foreign Armada."

Rosalia tried to imagine either man in a legitimate profession, captaining their own ship. "Please do. After what they've been through, one or both of them may be prepared for a new life that doesn't risk their necks or their hands on the chopping blocks."

"Excellent." Elurin bowed to her. "It has been my honor to make your acquaintance, Rosalia. Enjoy your time aboard my ship and never hesitate to come to me should you encounter any troubles. I'm easy to find."

After they parted ways, Xavier led her down below one level and opened a door to a small stateroom with a bed against one wall draped in sage green sheets, two oversized pillows at the head.

The moment he shut the door behind them, Rosalia shot Xavier a look. "How did you pull this off?"

"I told you, I have friends in high places."

Rosalia resisted the itch on her palms, a dire urge to slap the smug expression off his handsome face. Damn him for looking so attractive and arrogant. And bless him for being there when they needed him, even if he did have ulterior motives like using her to regain the mirror. "I don't mean that," she murmured, voice barely a whisper. "I mean, I know from experience of riding on your back that dragons can fly swiftly, but how did you get to Ilyria in time to have a ship meet us at sea?"

"Another secret of the hoard." When she crossed her arms, he added, "I'll show you once we're home."

Home? She didn't get to question it, because he turned down the bed and gestured with a palm. "You must be tired."

"I am, but I have a suitable bed on the *Sword*, Xavier. Or should I call you… Zaviriel?"

He grimaced. "Please don't."

"Going to tell me the story behind that one?"

"Only if you take a rest. I can't imagine the past few days were easy wrangling a couple dozen thieves into makeshift sailors. You look tired, and for the job we have to do, tired won't be enough."

"I *am* tired."

"Then take a rest and let Elurin's crew handle it. It's smooth sailing from here on out, literally and figuratively."

Giving in to his polite demands, Rosalia settled on the edge of the bed. It shifted beneath her hands, and the moment she stretched out along it, all the energy fled her tired limbs until it felt like her bones had melted into water.

He hadn't been lying about the comfort of an elven bed. The ones in his hoard were Saudonian by design and satisfying, but the mattress in his cabin may as well have been fashioned from clouds and magic, the physical embodiment of affluence. A quiet moan of relief escaped her before she could swallow it back. Too much time had passed since she'd been able to sleep without worries or pressing concerns weighing down on her. First, she'd been taken prisoner and sent to her death, and then it'd been days of worry for her fellow thieves and mourning for the murdered.

"I thought you'd feel that way."

Damn his smug face. "You can have your bed back in a moment."

"I'm fine bunking down on the floor for a while if it means you'll be in top form again."

Rosalia sighed. "You won't bunk down on the floor. I'm only resting my eyes. Besides... there's... enough room for... for two. Gods, this bed."

A few moments of silence passed, and suddenly her eyes were opening to a dim cabin lit only by moonlight and a single pale amber stone glowing in the distant upper corner of the cabin beside the door. The bedside lantern on the table had been extinguished, and there was silence all around except for the gentle lap of water against the hull. She'd been swaddled within a fine elven blanket that smelled like sunshine, her leggings and leather shirt removed, leaving her in only a thin cotton chemise and her undergarments.

And then there was a warm man behind her, the heat of him searing across her back through a layer of wool. That persistent aroma of smoke and forest surrounded her in a haze, enveloping her senses.

She shifted. "Xavier?"

He stirred. "Huh?"

"Just making sure it was you," she lied lamely. Who else would it be?

A moment of silence passed, the awkward lull of a few heartbeats. "Apologies. I meant to lay down for a moment, and I suppose the same exhaustion overcame me as well." He shifted, as if preparing to rise.

"No. No, it's fine. It's your bed after all, and there *is* plenty of room for two."

Although he hadn't slid beneath the sheets and what had to be the finest jasmora wool blanket she'd ever touched even during her nights of second-story work in Enimura, he was close enough for the gesture of lying beside her to feel personal. He looked uncomfortable there, and if his heat wasn't radiating through the short distance between them, she would have thought him to be chilly.

"Are you sure?"

"It's only a bed, and you can't be comfortable sleeping on all of this jasmora. It's designed to be on *top* of you."

Rosalia twisted around to face him and tugged the sheets until Xavier repositioned, allowing her to drag both layers over his body. Then they were beneath it together, trapping that lovely smell of man and dragon in close quarters. It had become something of an addiction in the recent days of their acquaintance.

She watched the rise and fall of his chest beneath the blanket, his dark hair an ink black spill over the linen pillowcase. Guests aboard elven ships slept in luxury, leading her to wonder if the officers' quarters were just as fine, if not better?

And then he moved nearer, breeching the narrow strip of no-man's-land until there was no space between them. Her pulse galloped in her chest, because she couldn't imagine anything but what it would be like if there weren't so many clothes separating them too.

20

LETTING GO

THOSE THREE DAYS OF SEPARATION HAD BEEN maddening, Xavier spending all the while wondering if Rosalia was safe and sound. From the moment he saw her aboard the *Noble Sword*, the wind tossing her brown hair and the evening sun setting her features aglow with golden warmth, he'd wanted nothing more than to take her in his arms.

He'd wanted to kiss her, wanted to promise to never part from her again.

For three days, he'd paced the deck of the *Opal Destiny* while Elurin poked holes through his story and made fun of his claims that his and Rosalia's relationship was merely platonic, a means to an end to recover the Eyeglass.

Platonic relationship indeed.

So platonic she dominated his thoughts when they were apart, and the phantom of her scent hung in the air so heavy he thought he'd smelled hints of smoke and desert while standing in the middle of the damned open sea.

She didn't resist the arm he slid around her middle beneath the blankets, or that he drew her closer against him and basked in the sweet smell of her hair. Her breaths quickened.

"What are you doing?"

"You shivered," he said.

Xavier waited for her to throw his arm away. She didn't. Instead, she pressed nearer and turned her face against his throat just beneath his chin. Her thumb skimmed his cheek and swept over his jawline, gliding over the dark stubble emerging since long before he left for the elven lands. He hadn't used a razor since Rosalia came into his home, not that it was often needed, his hair growth proportionate to his slow aging.

"I didn't think elves grew beards."

"You know that I'm not an elf."

"Mm. You said technically you're not an elf, you're a weredragon. Werewolves are men or elves who turn into wolves, so I assume you're an elf who turns into a dragon."

He grunted.

"Or do all weredragons have pointed ears?" Her finger trailed up to his ear and slid over the tapered tip. He suppressed a shiver.

"Suddenly curious about my kind?"

"Very. You speak little of them." She leaned back and peered at him in the dim light, although he could see her without suffering any loss in vision. Her eyes danced with warmth and humor, a hint of mischief visible in her smile. "Anyway, I think I prefer you like this. The scruffiness looks good on you." She caressed again, rubbing the pad of her thumb back and forth, teasing the same ear before her touch returned to his face.

Xavier couldn't wait another moment. Couldn't delay. Claiming her mouth became his only priority in that moment. So he did.

The second their lips met, a spark traveled through him, a jolt of lightning in the chest sizzling down every nerve ending. She tasted like light and life and sunlight, and so many sweet things he hadn't thought one kiss could convey, her mouth suffusing his taste buds with a flavor he'd compare to heaven.

At first, she made a noise of surprise, but then her fingers curled against his shoulder, the other hand buried in his hair and anchoring him in place. Her lips parted to him, eager and feverish, a sweep of her tongue exploring his mouth with mounting enthusiasm.

He kissed her again, over and over, each time as satisfying as the last, even as his mind drifted to a dozen other places he'd prefer to kiss next.

It was the kiss he'd wanted that night in the gardens, the kiss he'd needed after rescuing her from a wagon destined for her execution, a kiss he'd craved since the first moment she emerged from his spare bedroom covered head to toe in silk.

And he ended it there, drawing away, because when he made love to her, he wanted the moment to be sheer perfection. Her eyes remained lidded, features drowsy despite the satisfied smile on her face.

"About time," she murmured.

"Just warming up."

"Mm... I like your idea of a warmup then." Her hand smoothed across his chest, absently petting and stroking the contours of his pectoral muscles. "Thank you, by the way. I didn't get much of a chance to say it earlier, but thank you for bringing the elves to us."

"You're welcome."

"So, are you going to tell me why you looked mad enough to spit fire earlier?"

"I did not."

"Mm-hmm. Were you by chance... upset Elurin was flirting with me." When Xavier said nothing, she continued. "That's it, isn't it?"

"I don't have any claim to you and absolutely no reason to deny someone else the privilege."

"That isn't answering my question. I asked if you were upset to see someone else flirting with me."

Damn her for possessing acute observational skills. Xavier grunted again. "A little."

Her lips brushed over his, laughter alight on his mouth. "Was that so difficult to admit?"

"No," he confessed.

"Thank you."

Was it possible she'd truly been attracted to him after all on the day she'd come into his shop hunting for the mirror? The look in her eyes was pure feminine interest, the kind of expression he'd seen time and time again upon many young ladies entranced by his wealth and physical features they considered to be exotic.

He cupped a handful of her bottom and squeezed. Undressing Rosalia for bed had been an exercise in masochism, though he'd stripped her no more than required to appreciate the soft wool blanket for a restful night of sleep. He hadn't wanted his first appreciative glimpses of her body to be while she lay unconscious, recuperating after a harrowing escape. He wanted her to be awake, aware, and smoldering with unrestrained passion.

She kissed him again, providing all the encouragement he needed to make that moment now. With the hand molded to her warm cheek, he coaxed her leg over his hip, parting her thighs enough for an upward stroke of his fingers to find the narrow strip of cloth between them. When his thumb brushed against her, she jerked and clutched his arm with one hand.

"Xavier?"

He stilled. Had he misread her, imagined something that wasn't there? Another glance at Rosalia's face eased his worries when he saw her watching him hungrily. He moved his fingers in a long stroke and delighted when her dark eyes slit with pleasure and a low moan shuddered from her parted lips. "Yes?"

"What are you...? What are you doing?"

It wasn't a literal question. He knew as much, but he couldn't help the low chuckle that rumbled in his throat. "Do you want me to stop?"

Her fingers gripped his wrist. A moment passed before she answered with a strangled, "No. Gods, no."

He dragged the little scrap of feminine undergarment down then returned his fingers where they belonged, gliding against her bare skin, the silken smoothness of her inner thighs, and finally the sweet spot between them. She parted for him, wet and eager, the warmth of her body his to claim with a skilled play of his fingers.

In decades of existence, he'd never had an erection throb so feverish and stiff, beckoning him to take his pleasure and join her body for shared ecstasy. He resisted, and through willpower he'd never possessed before, he ignored the mating call urging him to claim her.

Two fingers delved anew. She sighed, twisted, and raised her hips. He met her and punctuated her rhythm with a stroke of his thumb against the tender center of her, against the little button that drove her wild and reduced her to writhing against the sheets.

The moment he bunched her camisole up around her ribs, exposing the bottom of her breasts, his mouth ached for one taste of them. "Let go," he beckoned, bowing over her and dragging the thin cotton up with his teeth to reveal plump breasts capped with tawny, reddish-brown nipples. He caressed one with his other hand and circled his thumb over its tip. It puckered in response, then he took the tightly budded peak captive between his lips.

She tugged his hair and guided him to the other breast. He repeated the favor there, tracing the sensitive tip and rasping it with the edge of his teeth, teasing until she clenched around his fingers. Her breath quickened.

When he brushed the perfect sweet spot, her hips shot up off the bed and began to ride his hand in earnest, faster and harder than before while she made the most wonderful sounds of pure feminine ecstasy.

"Let go, Rosa." Then he kissed her one more time, as addicted to her taste as he was to the scent of her—the wild, sweet scent of smoke and desert wind enriching the smell of elvish wood and the salted sea.

When release crashed over her in the next moments, Xavier knew nothing could be more satisfying than the jubilant cry of his name from her lips.

21

FREE

Xavier wasn't present when she awakened in his stateroom the next morning. He'd drawn the blankets over her and crept out like a thief in the night, more covert than he gave himself credit for despite his claims of having no talent for subterfuge and stealth.

All the better perhaps. She tried to forget the satisfying moment of intimacy between them, but her mind betrayed her and drew a perfect, flawless recollection of his skilled fingers between her thighs.

Get it together, girl. More important things to handle right now. Priorities in mind, she donned her leggings and pulled on the leather shirt Xavier had removed.

There was too much distance between the two ships for her to cross over by gangplank, but the amicable elves dropped a boat and rowed her over, no qualms, no complaint, merry smiles and pleasant service.

She arrived on the *Noble Sword* to find there were still elves aboard the ship, an abundance of their crewmen taking over the day-to-day activities expected of sailors. Linen and clothing hung on lines stretched across the berth, and the aroma of a hearty, elvish stew greeted her when she popped into the galley. Jabari and Enrikos, sat at a table together, shoveling soup into their mouths. She joined them and ate until her belly was full to bursting.

Enrikos belched and wiped his mouth with his wrist. "Them elves sure know how to make a proper meal, don't they?"

Rosalia sighed and dragged a piece of crusty, still warm bread against the inside of her empty bowl. "They sure do. Now, either of you up to running a little errand for me?"

"Me!" Jabari shouted, jumping up.

"I can do it," the other said.

"You both can do it, if you want. I need you to gather everyone who isn't in their sickbed recovering. Pull 'em down to the berth for a chat. I have great news."

Enrikos nodded, his small face stoic. "You can count on me."

She piled their empty bowls and deposited them into the wash basin before jogging to the berth. A couple of the thieves were already present, sprawled across cots or lying in hammocks strung between the portholes. Sergei, Pachenzo, and Luca were playing dice, the fourth player of their game an elven marine with brawny, golden brown arms covered in tattoos. The dice belonged to him obviously, as they were pale cream bone, polished smooth with elvish characters and numbers on the glossy surfaces.

Luca rose and beckoned her over. "Hey, Rosalia. Come to play a game with us?"

"Not right now. I'm calling together a meeting to relay some good news."

Pachenzo swept the dice up from the floor and straightened. "How good is the news?"

"Positively fantastic."

"Better than his luck then," the elven marine said, chuckling. "I'll take this as my cue to head out. And before you try to pocket my dice—it's fine. Keep them."

Pachenzo scowled at first, until he realized the elf had given him the dice. "Really?"

"I have more. Besides, you could use the luck, friend. Take them with my blessing." He bowed then strode away, ascending through an open hatch nearby to the main deck.

"I see you boys are making friends."

Sergei chuckled. "They're nice people. Now, what is this news?"

"I'll tell you soon."

One at a time, the rest of the able-bodied entered from different corners of the ship, some of them standing with their arms crossed and others sitting on crates and boxes to wait.

"All right. I think that's about everyone who can get out of bed. So, I spoke with the captain of the *Opal Destiny*, and he's a good guy. He and my friend assure me that there's a place for all of us in Ilyria if we want it. The elvish Thieves Guild and Grandmaster Nemuria will be happy to have us if you can follow her rules."

"What kind of rules?" Sergei asked.

"I don't know. I suppose we'll find out when we get there. Every Thieves Guild is going to have some home rules that vary, so I understand if you want to take a little while to consider it."

Luca snorted. "As long as the basics are the same, consider me in. A few days ago, we were destined to sail toward slavery."

"And now we have a fresh start," Soraya said, pinning him beneath a meaningful, long-lasting gaze that made Rosalia wonder about the nature of their relationship.

Several heads nodded, raising her confidence another notch. Rosalia grinned easily. "Better than raising the black flag and sailing seas with unknown naval dangers, now isn't it? Everyone knows pirates are out of luck when it comes to guild protection."

When a few glances settled on Pachenzo, he scowled and kicked a crate. "I get it, damn. I'm sorry for running my mouth."

"Water under the bridge. Now, when we arrive, I'll speak with Grandmaster Nemuria and find out her rules. I'm sure there's other arrangements to be made if no one wants to continue steal—"

"The fuck else would we do?" Horatio belted out, voice thundering against the wooden bulkheads. "Thieving's in our blood."

"Damn right it is," another thief agreed.

"What about you, Rosalia? Will you be leading a gang of your own?" Jabari asked.

"Me?" The thought had never occurred to her, too much responsibility attached to the role of a gang leader, down to meting out discipline to errant thieves who failed to obey the rules. She'd have to collect taxes, assign jobs, and meet with the grandmaster on a regular basis.

The lives of her gang would be in her hands, up to her to deal with the city watchmen, or whatever equivalent existed in Ilyria. She shivered at the thought of holding a candid discussion with a guard to determine how much money he'd need to look the other way.

She'd have to learn elvish politics.

If there was even a minute spark of interest, the idea of learning politics dampened it—*drowned* it.

"No. Too much work."

"Aww," Jabari said.

Enrikos's face fell. "I wanted first dibs on your gang."

"Sorry, kids. I'll help you find a good gang to join, but I'm not leading anyone. Hell, I don't even know if I'm staying in Ilyria after this."

The meeting broke apart soon after that. From the berth, she spread the news to the ailing and injured in the officers' quarters, then took a hatch to the main deck.

"Rosalia!" Enrikos called out.

"What is it?"

His shrewd eyes studied her, too old and intelligent to be in a face so young. "You're going back to Saudonia, aren't you?"

"I am."

"To Enimura?"

She bit her tongue, reluctant to whisper a word of the meticulous plan she and Xavier had created. "Possibly, at some point I imagine I will."

His solemn expression never changed. He pushed a rolled sheet of parchment into her hands. "Then you'll need this to learn the Rat Ways if you want to move around the city safely. We're not supposed to tell anyone who isn't a Rat, but I trust you. I found this in the captain's quarters and sketched out everything you need to know."

Rosalia unrolled a map of the city, a fine depiction of it drawn by a professional hand. Over it, Enrikos had scrawled several lines and notes, revealing the many sewer lines and passages beneath the city.

Due to their knowledge of the vast underground system beneath Enimura, the Sewer Rats had been one of the only gangs to escape the hangman's noose. Enrikos kept her captivated with his version of the events that night, describing how they escaped the city via an abandoned well in Old Enimura, the poverty-stricken district at the southwestern outskirts of the city where the watchmen never patrolled.

Years ago, when the city had undergone reconstruction, Old Enimura had been passed over, deemed unworthy of the thousands of gold spent to erect a massive wall around the rest of Enimura. Deemed unworthy of protection, of love, of safety, and anything resembling human decency. The children had all escaped the city via the sewers by crawling through an opening joined to the forgotten well, and they'd emerged in Old Enimura, the only region excluded from the purge.

Suddenly aware of a major oversight in the crown's otherwise flawless plan, she wondered why there had been no raids in that district. Had it been the lack of gangs based in the area, or had the watch shown pity, deciding not to risk razing the battered, crumbling shacks of poor citizens unable to rub two copper ramirans together?

No. The watch had no pity, nor did the crown. She doubted it had been intentional.

Later, she'd discuss it with Xavier.

"Where did they go after escaping by the well?"

"We were going to head west to Clovera. The desert is cold at night sometimes, but we've all been without homes so long we know the best places to hide. Especially during the heat of day."

"And once in Clovera?"

"Say we're orphans, of course. We all had different stories, so we were going to stagger our arrivals. Only one of us old enough to pass as an adult is Calan, so he was going to find honest work as a boot polisher. Then adopt some of us."

She listened to the rest of the Rats' master plan, nodding.

By the conclusion, Enrikos was nibbling his lower lip. "Do you think they're all safe? I got pinched because I went back to look for a friend who didn't check in at our lair."

"Did you find your friend?"

"No, didn't see her." A tearful head shake followed, moisture glistening in his brown eyes against dark lashes before spilling over freckled cheeks. A child his age should have been at home learning his numbers, reading history, and helping his mum with chores around the house instead of crawling through muck in the sewers.

But they were the Rats because they had no mums and fathers, a life on the streets preferred over the laws of an orphanage with an unforgiving governess.

"I bet she turned up just after you left."

"I hope so."

"And I bet the others are in Clovera right now, hoping you join them soon. I'll visit the orphanage there personally."

"You will?" He jumped, eyes bright and eager. He stumbled forward and threw his skinny arms around her waist, burying his face against her stomach.

What could she do but hug him in return?

———

Xavier and Elurin had been standing on the quarter-deck of the *Destiny* when Rosalia emerged from below and crossed over to the other ship.

"She isn't human," Elurin said suddenly.

Feigning disinterest, Xavier examined his nails. "Why do you say that?"

"I can see it in her. The way she walks. Her stance.

There's magic shimmering around the core of her soul like smoldering coals."

"Stop looking at her damn soul."

"But it's such a pretty thing. Like star rubies lit from behind by a candle flame."

Xavier said nothing.

"Though, I have to say, the rest of her is also beautiful. She'll make a breathtaking addition to the Valanyan Thieves Guild. I daresay, Nemuria would want to keep her as a leader of sorts, with that kind of unrefined power lurking inside her."

"If you're trying to make me jealous—"

Elurin chuckled. "Trying? You wear your heart on your sleeve. Don't forget that I know what you've been after. What you're searching for. Have you told her yet, or have you merely kept her in the dark like a clueless child?"

"I plan to tell her in time. Once this rubbish with the mirror is handled. When all is finished there, once the mirror is once again in safe hands, I'll tell her how I feel."

"Good." Elurin glanced at him sidelong, a fair brow raised. "Do you truly think she can help replenish your race?"

Xavier watched the elves in the distance. They lowered a rope to Rosalia and pulled her to the deck of the ship. Safe. "My mother was a mage, but there wasn't enough magic coursing through her to carry me to the end of her pregnancy. She nearly lost me twice," he said in a quiet voice. "My father said it was the most terrifying time of his life, how he couldn't sleep and spent his nights watching her—watching us, petrified every kick was my death or hers. She suffered so much to bring me into this world. Only for her body to give out on her anyway years later."

Longer silence passed between them. Elurin rested a hand on Xavier's back. When he spoke, nothing but compassion filled his voice. "In that case, I hope you find in her what you have sought all this time, friend. Gods know you've waited long enough to claim the one for you."

————

Hi, readers! I hope you enjoyed the hell out of the beginning to Rosalia's journey. It was one hell of a ride getting here. I adore her and Xavier so much, that I put this story off multiple times until it was just right.

Fool's Gold will be the next novel in the *Daughter of Fortune* series, available sometime in November!

If you loved it, please let me know.

Don't miss out out by signing up to my newsletter where I promise never to spam you and to only keep you updated on upcoming novels by me.

ABOUT THE AUTHOR

Domino Taylor is one-half of the pen name Vivienne Savage. This is her debut as a solo author and her first complete, unassisted work.

 facebook.com/Taylor.Author

twitter.com/msvsavage

instagram.com/msvsavage

CPSIA information can be obtained
at www.ICGtesting.com
Printed in the USA
LVHW042319030423
743399LV00018B/588

9 780578 410128